D1309957

VENOMOUS TALES OF VILLAINY AND VENGEANCE

ALSO EDITED BY HELEN HOKE

A CHILLING COLLECTION

DEMONIC, DANGEROUS AND DEADLY

DEMONS WITHIN

EERIE, WEIRD AND WICKED

GHOSTLY, GRIM AND GRUESOME

MYSTERIOUS, MENACING AND MACABRE

SINISTER, STRANGE AND SUPERNATURAL

SPOOKS, SPOOKS, SPOOKS

TALES OF FEAR AND FRIGHTENING PHENOMENA

THRILLERS, CHILLERS AND KILLERS

TERRORS, TORMENTS AND TRAUMAS

UNCANNY TALES OF UNEARTHLY AND UNEXPECTED HORRORS

WEIRDIES, WEIRDIES, WEIRDIES

WITCHES, WITCHES, WITCHES

VENOMOUS TALES OF VILLAINY AND VENGEANCE

An V anthology by Helen Hoke

Lodestar Books
E. P. Dutton   New York

No character in this book is intended to represent any actual person; all the incidents of the story are entirely fictional in nature.

Copyright © 1984 by Helen Hoke

First published in England 1984 by J. M. Dent & Sons, Ltd

Published in the United States by E. P. Dutton, Inc.,
2 Park Avenue, New York, N.Y. 10016

Published simultaneously in Canada by
Fitzhenry & Whiteside Limited, Toronto

All rights reserved. No part of this publication may be reproduced or transmitted in any form or by any means, electronic or mechanical, including photocopying, recording, or any information storage and retrieval system now known or to be invented, without permission in writing from the publisher, except by a reviewer who wishes to quote brief passages in connection with a review written for inclusion in a magazine, newspaper, or broadcast.

Library of Congress Cataloging in Publication Data

Main entry under title:

Venomous tales of villainy and vengeance.

   "Lodestar books."
   Contents: John Charrington's wedding / E. Nesbit—
Skeleton / Ray Bradbury— Bronze / W.M. Tidmarsh—
[etc.]
   1. Horror tales, American. 2. Horror tales, English.
[1. Horror stories. 2. Short stories] 1. Hoke, Helen,

PZ5.V44 1984 [Fic] 84–8065
ISBN 0–525–67158–7

Editor: Virginia Buckley

Printed in England COBE First Edition

10 9 8 7 6 5 4 3 2 1

ACKNOWLEDGMENTS

The selections in this book are used by permission of and special arrangements with the proprietors of their respective copyrights, who are listed below. The editor's and publisher's thanks go to all who have made this collection possible.

The editor and publisher have made every effort to trace ownership of all material contained herein. It is their belief that the necessary permissions from publishers, authors, and authorized agents have been obtained in all cases. In the event of any questions arising as to the use of any material, the editor and publisher express regret for any error unconsciously made and will be pleased to make the necessary corrections in future editions of the book

"As Is," by Robert Silverberg. Reprinted by permission of the author and the author's agent, Kirby McCauley, Ltd.

"Bronze," by W. M. Tidmarsh. Reprinted by permission of *Short Stories Magazine*.

"Did You See the Window-cleaner?" by John Edgell. Reprinted from *John Edgell's Ghosts* by John Edgell, published by Wayland (Publishers) Ltd 1970, with the kind permission of the Publisher.

"The Hungry House," by Robert Bloch. © 1951 by Greenleaf Publishing Co. Renewed 1979 by Robert Bloch. Reprinted by permission of the author and the Scott Meredith Literary Agency Inc., 845 Third Avenue, New York, NY 10022, U.S.A.

"Skeleton," by Ray Bradbury. Copyright © 1945 by Ray Bradbury, renewed 1973. Reprinted by permission of Don Congdon Associates, Inc.

"The Skylight," by Penelope Mortimer. First published in *Saturday Lunch with the Brownings* by Penelope Mortimer, Hutchinson 1960.

"Smell," by Joan Aiken. Copyright © 1969 by Joan Aiken. From *A Bundle of Nerves* by Joan Aiken, published by Victor Gollancz Ltd. Reprinted by permission of Brandt & Brandt Literary Agents Inc., and Victor Gollancz Ltd.

POP.

MAY 1985

3 1172 01471 0107

CONTENTS

ABOUT THIS BOOK

In these eight shiver-provoking tales, characters are besieged by uncontrollable forces and take part in a play for which the script grows more terrifying with each turn of the page. All of the stories were written by star authors and have been selected carefully to assure that you will be held spellbound by the performance, wondering, as the lights flood the stage, what inexplicable horrors lurk in the wings.

Here is a preview of the scenes that are about to unfold.

The stage is set for a most unusual union in E. Nesbit's "John Charrington's Wedding," which the groom has promised to attend—dead or alive.

In Ray Bradbury's "Skeleton," the leading man can't stand the thought of those awful fibulas and femurs, carpales and phalanges, rattling around inside him. His obsessive battle with the thing beneath his skin will chill your own bones.

A scaly, dragonlike statue is the central prop in "Bronze" by W. M. Tidmarsh. Genial-looking when viewed from above, somehow the model looks sinister, even menacing, at eye level.

And what is the strange, bronze-colored rash spreading on the skin of the statue's new owner?

Robert Silverberg brings us the humorous tale of a car that must be taken as is, even with a mysterious trunk that won't open—until it is needed. The memorable trip in this car will be certain to provoke chuckles from those who go along for the ride.

In "Smell" by Joan Aiken, a highly independent, elderly woman seeks to avenge the theft of her savings by using her keenest remaining sense. She proves herself to be quite capable in her role of sleuth, with an unusual method of crime detection—and punishment.

A strange old house is the setting of "The Hungry House" by Robert Bloch. From the very first night in their new home, a couple notices that their reflections are distorted in mirrors and windowpanes—something *alien* is looking back at them. And that is just when the terror begins.

In John Edgell's "Did You See the Window-cleaner?" Craddock must have the cleanest windows in the city. The window-cleaner comes every day with his buckets and cloth. But why has no one else seen him seated on the rickety wooden cradle suspended outside the building?

When she lets her child crawl into the skylight of a boarded up, desolate vacation home, a woman knows she has made a dreadful mistake. But there is no turning back in this masterful tale by Penelope Mortimer.

Take your seats. The horrifying show is about to begin, and the spotlight will fall on evil itself.

Helen Hoke

VENOMOUS TALES OF VILLAINY AND VENGEANCE

JOHN CHARRINGTON'S WEDDING

E. NESBIT

No one ever thought that May Forster would marry John Charrington; but he thought differently, and things which John Charrington intended had a queer way of coming to pass. He asked her to marry him before he went up to Oxford. She laughed and refused him. He asked her again next time he came home. Again she laughed, tossed her dainty blonde head, and again refused. A third time he asked her; she said it was becoming a confirmed bad habit, and laughed at him more than ever.

John was not the only man who wanted to marry her: She was the belle of our village coterie, and we were all in love with her more or less; it was a sort of fashion, like heliotrope ties or Inverness capes. Therefore we were as much annoyed as surprised when John Charrington walked into our little local Club—we held it in a loft over the saddler's, I remember—and invited us all to his wedding.

"Your wedding?"

"You don't mean it?"

"Who's the happy fair? When's it to be?"

John Charrington filled his pipe and lighted it before he replied. Then he said, "I'm sorry to deprive you fellows of your only joke—but Miss Forster and I are to be married in September."

"You don't meant it?"

"He's got the boot again, and it's turned his head."

"No," I said, rising, "I see it's true. Lend me a pistol someone—or a first-class fare to the other end of Nowhere. Charrington has bewitched the only pretty girl in our twenty-mile radius. Was it mesmerism, or a love potion, Jack?"

"Neither, sir, but a gift you'll never have—perseverance—and the best luck a man ever had in this world."

There was something in his voice that silenced me, and all the chaff of the other fellows failed to draw him further.

The queer thing about it was that when we congratulated Miss Forster, she blushed and smiled and dimpled, for all the world as though she were in love with him, and had been in love with him all the time. Upon my word, I think she had. Women are strange creatures.

We were all asked to the wedding. In Brixham everyone who was anybody knew everybody else who was anyone. My sisters were, I truly believe, more interested in the trousseau than the bride herself, and I was to be best man. The coming marriage was much canvassed at afternoon tea-tables, and at our little Club over the saddler's, and the question was always asked: "Does she care for him?"

I used to ask that question myself in the early days of their engagement, but after a certain evening in August I never asked it again. I was coming home from the Club through the churchyard. Our church is on a thyme-grown hill, and the turf about it is so thick and soft that one's footsteps are noiseless.

I made no sound as I vaulted the low lichened wall and threaded my way between the tombstones. It was at the same instant that I heard John Charrington's voice, and saw her. May was sitting on a low flat gravestone, her face turned towards the full splendor of the western sun. Its expression ended, at once and for ever, any question of love for him; it was transfigured to a beauty I should not have believed possible, even to that beautiful little face.

John lay at her feet, and it was his voice that broke the stillness of the golden August evening. "My dear, my dear, I believe I should come back from the dead if you wanted me!"

I coughed at once to indicate my presence, and passed on into the shadow, fully enlightened.

The wedding was to be early in September. Two days before I had to run up to town on business. The train was late, of course, for we are on the South-eastern, and as I stood grumbling with my watch in my hand, whom should I see but John Charrington and May Forster. They were walking up and down the unfrequented end of the platform, arm in arm, looking into each other's eyes, careless of the sympathetic interest of the porters.

Of course I knew better than to hesitate a moment before burying myself in the booking-office, and it was not till the train drew up at the platform, that I obtrusively passed the pair with my suitcase and took the corner in a first-class smoking-carriage. I did this with as good an air of not seeing them as I could assume. I pride myself on my discretion, but if John was travelling alone I wanted his company. I had it.

"Hullo, old man," came his cheery voice as he swung his bag into my carriage. "Here's luck; I was expecting a dull journey!"

"Where are you off to?" I asked, discretion still bidding me turn my eyes away, though I felt, without looking, that hers were red-rimmed.

"To old Branbridge's," he answered, shutting the door and leaning out for a last word with his sweetheart.

"Oh, I wish you wouldn't go, John," she was saying in a low, earnest voice. "I feel certain something will happen."

"Do you think I should let anything happen to keep me, and the day after tomorrow our wedding-day?"

"Don't go," she answered, with a pleading intensity which would have sent my suitcase onto the platform and me after it. But she wasn't speaking to me. John Charrington was made differently; he rarely changed his opinions, never his resolutions.

He only stroked the little ungloved hands that lay on the carriage door.

"I must, May. The old boy's been awfully good to me, and now he's dying I must go and see him, but I shall come home in time for—" The rest of the parting was lost in a whisper and in the rattling lurch of the starting train.

She spoke as the train moved: "You're sure to come?"

"Nothing shall keep me," he answered; and we steamed out. After he had seen the last of the little figure on the platform, he leaned back in his corner and kept silence for a minute.

When he spoke it was to explain to me that his godfather, whose heir he was, lay dying at Peasmarsh Place, some fifty miles away, and had sent for John, and John had felt bound to go.

"I shall surely be back tomorrow," he said, "or, if not, the day after, in heaps of time. Thank Heaven, one hasn't to get up in the middle of the night to get married nowadays!"

"And suppose Mr. Branbridge dies?"

"Alive or dead I mean to be married on Thursday!" John answered, lighting a cigar and unfolding *The Times*.

At Peasmarsh station we said good-bye, and he got out, and I saw him ride off; I went on to London, where I stayed the night.

When I got home the next afternoon, a very wet one, by the way, my sister Fanny greeted me with: "Where's Mr. Charrington?"

"Goodness knows," I answered testily. Every man, since Cain, has resented that kind of question.

"I thought you might have heard from him," she went on, "as you're to give him away tomorrow."

"Isn't he back?" I asked, for I had confidently expected to find him at home.

"No, Geoffrey"—my sister Fanny always had a way of jumping to conclusions, especially such conclusions as were least favorable to her fellow-creatures—"he has not returned, and, what is more, you may depend upon it he won't. You mark my words, there'll be no wedding tomorrow."

My sister Fanny has a power of annoying me which no other human being possesses.

"*You* mark *my* words," I retorted with asperity, "you had better give up making such a thundering idiot of yourself. There'll be more wedding tomorrow than ever you'll take the first part in." A prophecy which, by the way, came true.

But though I could snarl confidently to my sister, I did not feel so comfortable when late that night, I, standing on the doorstep of John's house, heard that he had not returned. I went home gloomily through the rain. Next morning brought a brilliant blue sky, gold sun, and all such softness of air and beauty of cloud as go to make up a perfect day. I woke with a vague feeling of having gone to bed anxious, and of being rather averse to facing that anxiety in the light of full wakefulness.

But with my shaving-water came a note from John which relieved my mind and sent me up to the Forsters' with a light heart.

May was in the garden. I saw her blue gown through the hollyhocks as the lodge gates swung to behind me. So I did not go up to the house, but turned aside down the turfed path.

"He's written to you too," she said, without preliminary greeting, when I reached her side.

"Yes, I'm to meet him at the station at three and come straight on to the church."

Her face looked pale, but there was a brightness in her eyes, and a tender quiver about the mouth that spoke of renewed happiness.

"Mr. Branbridge begged him so to stay another night that he had not the heart to refuse," she went on. "He is so kind, but I wish he hadn't stayed."

I was at the station at half past two. I felt rather annoyed with John. It seemed a sort of slight to the beautiful girl who loved him that he should come, as it were, out of breath, and with the dust of travel upon him, to take her hand, which some of us would have given the best years of our lives to take.

But when the three o'clock train glided in, and glided out again having brought no passengers to our little station, I was more than annoyed. There was no other train for thirty-five minutes; I calculated that, with much hurry, we might just get to the church in time for the ceremony; but, oh, what a fool to have missed that first train! What other man could have done it?

That thirty-five minutes seemed a year as I wandered around the station reading the advertisements and the time-tables, and the company's by-laws, and getting more and more angry with John Charrington. This confidence in his own power of getting everything he wanted the minute he wanted it was leading him too far. I hate waiting. Everyone does, but I believe I hate it more than anyone else. The three thirty-five was late, of course.

I ground my pipe between my teeth and stamped with impatience as I watched the signals. *Click*. The signal went down. Five minutes later I flung myself into the carriage that I had brought for John.

"Drive to the church!" I said as someone shut the door. "Mr. Charrington hasn't come by this train."

Anxiety now replaced anger. What had become of the man? Could he have been taken ill suddenly? I had never known him have a day's illness in his life. And even so he might have telegraphed. Some awful accident must have happened to him. The thought that he had played her false never—no, not for a moment—entered my head. Yes, something terrible had happened to him, and on me lay the task of telling his bride. I almost wished the carriage would upset and break my head so that someone else might tell her, not I, who— But that's nothing to do with this story.

It was five minutes to four as we drew up to the churchyard gate. A double row of eager onlookers lined the path from lych-gate to porch. I sprang from the carriage and passed up between them. Our gardener had a good place near the front door. I stopped.

"Are they waiting still, Byles?" I asked simply to gain time, for of course I knew they were by the waiting crowd's attentive attitude.

"Waiting, sir? No, no, sir; why, it must be over by now."

"Over! Then Mr. Charrington's come?"

"To the minute, sir; must have missed you somehow, and I say, sir," lowering his voice, "I never seen Mr. John the least bit so afore, but my opinion is he's been drinking pretty free. His clothes was all dusty and his face like a sheet. I tell you I didn't like the looks of him at all, and the folks inside are saying all sorts of things. You'll see, something's gone very wrong with Mr. John, and he's tried liquor. He looked like a ghost, and in he went with his eyes straight before him, with never a look or a word for none of us, him that was always such a gentleman!"

I had never heard Byles make so long a speech. The crowd in the churchyard were talking in whispers and getting ready rice and slippers to throw at the bride and bridegroom. The ringers were ready with their hands on the ropes to ring out the merry peal as the bride and bridegroom should come out.

A murmur from the church announced them; out they came. Byles was right. John Charrington did not look himself. There was dust on his coat, his hair was disarranged. He seemed to have been in some row, for there was a black mark above his eyebrow. He was deathly pale. But his pallor was not greater than that of the bride, who might have been carved in ivory—dress, veil, orange blossoms, face and all.

As they passed, the ringers stopped—there were six of them—and then, on the ears expecting the gay wedding peal, came the slow tolling of the passing bell.

A thrill of horror at so foolish a jest from the ringers passed through us all. But the ringers themselves dropped the ropes and fled like rabbits out of the church into the sunlight. The bride shuddered, and grey shadows came about her mouth, but the bridegroom led her on down the path where the people stood with the handfuls of rice; but the handfuls were never thrown, and the wedding-bells never rang. In vain the ringers were urged to remedy their mistake: They protested with many whispered expletives that they would see themselves further first.

In a hush like the hush in the chamber of death, the bridal pair passed into their carriage and its door slammed behind them.

Then the tongues were loosed. A babel of anger, wonder, and conjecture from the guests and the spectators.

"If I'd seen his condition, sir," said old Forster to me as we drove off, "I would have stretched him on the floor of the church, sir, by Heaven I would, before I'd have let him marry my daughter!"

Then he put his head out of the window.

"Drive like hell," he cried to the coachman. "Don't spare the horses."

He was obeyed. We passed the bride's carriage. I forbore to look at it, and old Forster turned his head away and swore. We reached home before it.

We stood in the hall doorway, in the blazing afternoon sun, and in about half a minute we heard wheels crunching the gravel. When the carriage stopped in front of the steps, old Forster and I ran down.

"Great Heaven, the carriage is empty! And yet—"

I had the door opened in a minute, and this is what I saw—no sign of John Charrington; only May, his wife, a huddled heap of white satin lying half on the floor of the carriage and half on the seat.

"I drove straight here, sir," said the coachman, as the bride's father lifted her out; "and I'll swear no one got out of the carriage."

We carried her into the house in her bridal dress and drew back her veil. I saw her face. Shall I ever forget it? White, white and drawn with agony and horror, bearing such a look of terror as I have never seen since except in dreams. And her hair, her radiant blonde hair, I tell you it was white as snow.

As we stood, her father and I, half mad with the horror and mystery of it, a boy came up the avenue—a telegraph boy. He brought the orange envelope to me. I tore it open.

Mr. Charrington was thrown from the dog-cart on his way to the station at half past one. Killed on the spot!

And he was married to May Forster in our parish church at *half past three*, in the presence of half the parish.

"Alive or dead I mean to be married!"

What had passed in that carriage on the homeward drive? No one knows—no one will ever know. Oh, May! Oh, my dear!

Before a week was over, they laid her beside her husband in our little churchyard on the thyme-covered hill—the churchyard where they had kept their love-trysts.

Thus was accomplished John Charrington's wedding.

SKELETON

RAY BRADBURY

It was past time for him to see the doctor again. Mr. Harris turned palely in at the stairwell, and on his way up the flight he saw Dr. Burleigh's name gilded over a pointing arrow. Would Dr. Burleigh sigh when he walked in? After all, this would make the tenth trip so far this year. But Burleigh shouldn't complain; after all, he was paid for the examinations!

The nurse looked Mr. Harris over and smiled, a bit amusedly, as she tiptoed to the glazed glass door, opened it, and put her head in. Harris thought he heard her say, "Guess who's here, Doctor?" And didn't the doctor's acid voice reply faintly, "Oh, my God, *again*?" Harris swallowed uneasily.

When Harris walked in, Dr. Burleigh snorted thinly. "Aches in your bones again! Ah!" He scowled at Harris and adjusted his glasses. "My dear Harris, you've been curried with the finest tooth combs and bacteria brushes known to science. You're only nervous. Let's see your fingers. Too many cigarettes. Let me smell your breath. Too much protein. Let's see your eyes. Not

11

enough sleep. My response? Go to bed, stop the protein, no smoking. Ten dollars, please."

Harris stood there, sulking.

The doctor glanced up from his papers. "*You* still here? You're a hypochondriac! That's *eleven* dollars, now."

"But why should my bones ache?" asked Harris.

Dr. Burleigh addressed him as if he were a child. "You ever had a sore muscle, and kept at it, irritating it, fussing with it, rubbing it? It gets worse, the more you bother it. Then you leave it alone and the pain vanishes. You realize you caused most of the soreness, yourself. Well, son, that's what's with you. Leave yourself alone. Take a dose of salts. Get out of here and take that trip to Phoenix you've stewed about for months. Do you good to travel!"

Five minutes later, Mr. Harris riffled through a classified phone directory at the corner druggist's. A fine lot of sympathy one got from blind fools like Burleigh! He passed his finger down a list of bone specialists, found one named M. Munigant. Munigant lacked an M.D., or any other academical lettering behind his name, but his office was conveniently near. Three blocks down, one block over . . .

M. Munigant, like his office, was small and dark. Like his office, he smelled of iodoform, iodine, and other odd things. He was a good listener, though, and listened with eager, shiny moves of his eyes, and when he talked to Harris, he had an accent and seemed to whistle every word, undoubtedly due to imperfect dentures. Harris told all.

M. Munigant nodded. He had seen cases like this before. The bones of the body. Man was not aware of his bones. Ah, yes, the bones. The skeleton. Most difficult. Something concerning an imbalance, an unsympathetic coordination between soul, flesh and bone. "Very complicated," softly whistled M. Munigant. Harris listened, fascinated. Now, *here* was a doctor who understood his illness! "Psychological," said M. Munigant. He moved swiftly, delicately to a dingy wall and rattled down half a dozen X rays and paintings of the human skeleton. He pointed at these. Mr. Harris must become aware of his problem, yes. He pointed at this and that bone, and these and those, and some others.

The pictures were quite awful. They had something of the grotesquerie and off-bounds horror of a Dali painting. Harris shivered.

M. Munigant talked on. Did Mr. Harris desire treatment for his bones?

"That all depends," said Harris.

M. Munigant could not help Harris unless Harris was in the proper mood. Psychologically, one had to *need* help, or the doctor was of no use. But (shrugging) M. Munigant would "try."

Harris lay on a table with his mouth open. The lights were switched off, the shades drawn. M. Munigant approached his patient.

Something touched Harris's tongue.

He felt his jawbones forced out. They cracked and made noises. One of those pictures on the dim wall seemed to leap. A violent shivering went through Harris and, involuntarily, his mouth snapped shut.

M. Munigant cried out. He had almost had his nose bitten off! It was no use. Now was not the time. M. Munigant raised the shades. He looked dreadfully disappointed. When Mr. Harris felt he could cooperate psychologically, when Mr. Harris really *needed* help and trusted M. Munigant to help him, then maybe something could be done. M. Munigant held out his little hand. In the meantime, the fee was only two dollars. Mr. Harris must begin to think. Here was a sketch for Mr. Harris to take home and study. It would acquaint him with his body. He must be aware of himself. He must be careful. Skeletons were strange, unwieldy things. M. Munigant's eyes glittered. Good day to Mr. Harris. Oh, and would he have a breadstick? He proffered a jar of long hard salty breadsticks to Harris, taking one himself to chew on, and saying that chewing breadsticks kept him in—ah—practice.

See you soon, Mr. Harris.

Mr. Harris went home.

The next day was Sunday. Mr. Harris started the morning by feeling all sorts of new aches and pains in his body. He spent some time glancing at the funny papers and then looking with new interest at the little painting, anatomically perfect, of a skeleton M. Munigant had given him.

His wife, Clarisse, startled him at dinner when she cracked her exquisitely thin knuckles, one by one, until he clapped his hands to his ears and cried, "Don't do that!"

The remainder of the day he quarantined himself in his room. Clarisse was seated at bridge in the living room with three other ladies, laughing and conversing. Harris himself spent his time fingering and weighing the limbs of his body with growing curiosity. After an hour of this, he suddenly stood up and called, "Clarisse!"

She had a way of dancing into any room, her body doing all sorts of soft, agreeable things to keep her feet from ever quite touching the nap of a rug. She excused herself from her friends and came to see him now, brightly. She found him reseated in a far corner and she saw that he was staring at that anatomical sketch. "Are you still brooding, darling?" she asked. "Please don't." She sat upon his knees.

Her beauty could not distract him, now, in his absorption. He juggled her lightness, he touched her kneecap, suspiciously. It seemed to move under her pale, glowing skin. "Is it supposed to do that?" he asked, sucking in his breath.

"Is what supposed to do what?" she laughed. "You mean my kneecap?"

"Is it supposed to run around on top of your knee that way?"

She experimented. "So it *does*," she marveled. "Well, now, so it does. Icky." She pondered. "No. On the other hand—it doesn't. It's only an optical illusion. I think. The skin moves over the bone; not vice versa. See?" She demonstrated.

"I'm glad yours slithers, too," he sighed. "I was beginning to worry."

"About what?"

He patted his ribs. "My ribs don't go all the way down, they stop *here*. And I found some confounded ones that dangle in midair!"

Beneath the curve of her small breasts, Clarisse clasped her hands.

"Of course, silly, everybody's ribs stop at a given point. And those funny little short ones are just floating ribs."

"I just hope they don't float around too much," he said, making an uneasy joke. Now he desired that his wife leave him, he had some important discovering to do with his own body and he didn't want her laughing at him.

"I'll feel all right," he said. "Thanks for coming in, dear."

"Any time," she said, kissing him, rubbing her small pink warm nose against his.

"I'll be damned!" He touched his nose with his fingers, then hers. "Did you ever realize that the nose bone only comes down so far and a lot of gristly tissue takes up from there on?"

She wrinkled hers. "So what?" And, dancing, she exited.

He felt the sweat rise from the pools and hollows of his face, forming a salten tide to flow down his cheeks. Next on the agenda was his spinal cord and column. He examined it in the same manner as he operated the numerous push buttons in his office, pushing them to summon the messenger boys. But, in these pushings of his spinal column, fear and terrors answered, rushed from a million doors in Mr. Harris's mind to confront and shake him. His spine felt awfully—bony. Like a fish, freshly eaten and skeletonized, on a china platter. He fingered the little rounded knobbins. "My God."

His teeth began to chatter. God Almighty, he thought, why haven't I realized it all these years? All these years I've gone around with a—*skeleton*—inside me! He saw his fingers blur before him, like motion films triply speeded in their quaking apprehension. How is it that we take ourselves so much for granted? How is it we never question our bodies and our being?

A skeleton. One of those jointed, snowy, hard things, one of those foul, dry, brittle, gouge-eyed, skull-faced, shake-fingered, rattling things that sway from neck chains in abandoned webbed closets, one of those things found on the desert all long and scattered like dice!

He stood upright, because he could not bear to remain seated. Inside me now, he grasped his stomach, his head, inside my head is a—skull. One of those curved carapaces which holds my brain like an electrical jelly, one of those cracked shells with the holes in front like two holes shot through it by a double-barreled shotgun! With its grottoes and caverns of bone, its rivetments and placements for my flesh, my smelling, my seeing, my hearing, my thinking! A skull, encompassing my brain, allowing it to exit through its brittle windows to see the outside world!

He wanted to dash into the bridge party, upset it, a fox in a chickenyard, the cards fluttering all around like chicken feathers bursting upward in clouds! He stopped himself only with a violent, trembling effort. Now, now, man, control yourself. This is a revelation. Take it for what it's worth, understand it, savor it. *But a skeleton!* screamed his subconscious. I won't stand for it. It's vulgar, it's terrible, it's frightening. Skeletons are horrors; they clink and tinkle and rattle in old castles, hung from oaken beams, making long, indolently rustling pendulums on the wind. . . .

"Darling, will you come in and meet the ladies?" called his wife's sweet, clear voice.

Mr. Harris stood up. His *skeleton* was holding him up. This thing inside him, this invader, this horror, was supporting his arms, legs, and head. It was like feeling just behind you someone who shouldn't be there. With every step he took, he realized how dependent he was upon this other Thing.

"Darling, I'll be with you in a moment," he called weakly. To himself he said, "Come on, now, brace up. You've got to go back

16

to work tomorrow. And Friday you've got to make that trip to Phoenix. It's a long drive. Hundreds of miles. Got to be in shape for that trip or you won't get Mr. Creldon to put his money into your ceramics business. Chin up, now."

Five minutes later he stood among the ladies, being introduced to Mrs. Withers, Mrs. Abblematt, and Miss Kirthy, all of whom had skeletons inside them but took it very calmly, because nature had carefully clothed the bare nudity of clavicle, tibia, and femur with breasts, thighs, calves, with coiffure and eyebrow satanic, with bee-stung lips and—*Lord!* shouted Mr. Harris inwardly—when they talk or eat, part of their skeleton shows—their *teeth!* I never thought of that.

"Excuse me," he said, and ran from the room only in time to drop his dinner among the petunias over the garden balustrade.

That night, seated on the bed as his wife undressed, he pared his toenails and fingernails scrupulously. These parts, too, were where his skeleton was showing, indignantly growing out. He must have muttered something concerning this theory, because next thing he knew his wife, in negligee, slithered on the bed, yawning, "Oh, darling, fingernails are *not* bone, they're only hardened skin growths."

He threw the scissors away with relief. "Glad to hear that. Feel better." He looked at the ripe curves of her, marveling. "I hope all people are made the same way."

"If you aren't the darnedest hypochondriac I ever saw," she said. She snuggled to him. "Come on. What's wrong? Tell mama."

"Something inside me," he said. "Something—I ate."

The next morning and all afternoon at his downtown office, Mr. Harris found that the sizes, shapes, and constructions of various bones in his body displeased him. At 10 A.M., he asked to feel Mr. Smith's elbow one moment. Mr. Smith obliged, but scowled suspiciously. And after lunch Mr. Harris asked to touch

Miss Laurel's shoulder blade and she immediately pushed herself back against him, purring like a kitten, shutting her eyes in the mistaken belief that he wished to examine a few other anatomical delicacies. "Miss Laurel!" he snapped. "Stop that!"

Alone, he pondered his neuroses. The war just over, the pressure of his work, the uncertainty of the future, probably had much to do with his mental outlook. He wanted to leave the office, get into his own business, for himself. He had more than a little talent at artistic things, had dabbled in ceramics and sculpture. As soon as possible he'd get over into Arizona and borrow that money from Mr. Creldon. It would build him his kiln and set up his own shop. It was a worry. What a case he was. But it was a good thing he had contacted M. Munigant, who had seemed to be eager to understand and help him. He would fight it out with himself, not go back to either Munigant or Dr. Burleigh unless he was forced to. The alien feeling would pass. He sat staring into nothing.

The alien feeling did not pass. It grew.

On Tuesday and Wednesday it bothered him terrifically that his outer dermis, epidermis, hair, and other appendages were of a high disorder, while the integumented skeleton of himself was a slick clean structure of efficient organization. Sometimes, in certain lights while his lips were drawn morosely downward, weighted with melancholy, he imagined he saw his skull grinning at him behind the flesh. *It had its nerve, it did!*

"Let go of me!" he cried. "Let go of me! You've caught me, you've captured me! My lungs, you've got them in a vise! Release them!"

He experienced violent gasps as if his ribs were pressing in, choking the breath from him.

"My brain, stop *squeezing* it!"

And terrible hot headaches caught his brain like a bivalve in the compressed clamp of skull bones.

"My vitals! All my organs, let them be, for God's sake! Stay

18

away from my heart!" His heart seemed to cringe from the fanning nearness of his ribs. Ribs like pale spiders crouched and fiddled with their prey.

Drenched with sweat, he lay upon the bed one night while Clarisse was out attending a Red Cross meeting. He tried to gather his wits again, always amid the conflict of his disorderly exterior and this cool calciumed thing inside him with all its exact symmetry.

His complexion: Wasn't it oily and lined with worry?

Observe the flawless, snow-white perfection of the skull.

His nose: Wasn't it too large?

Then observe the small tiny bones of the skull's nose before that monstrous nasal cartilage begins forming Harris's lopsided proboscis.

His body: Wasn't it a bit plump?

Well, then, consider the skeleton: so slender, so svelte, so economical of line and contour. Like exquisitely carved oriental ivory it is, perfected and thin as a reed.

His eyes: Weren't they protuberant and ordinary and numb looking?

Be so kind as to note the eye sockets of the skeleton's skull: so deep and rounded, somber, quiet, dark pools, all knowing, eternal. Gaze deeply into skull sockets and you never touch the bottom of their dark understanding with any plumb line. All irony, all sadism, all life, all everything is there in the cupped darkness.

Compare. Compare. Compare.

He raged for hours, glib and explosive. And the skeleton, ever the frail and solemn philosopher, quietly hung inside of Harris, saying not a word, quietly suspended like a delicate insect within a chrysalis, waiting and waiting.

Then it came to Harris.

"Wait a minute. Hold on a minute," he exclaimed. "You're helpless, too. I've got you, too. I can make you do anything I want you to! And you can't prevent it! I say put up your carpales, metacarpals, and phalanges and—*sswtt*—up they go, as I wave to someone!" He giggled.

"I order to the fibula and femur to locomote and *hup* two three four, *hup* two three four—we walk around the block. There."

Harris grinned.

"It's a fifty-fifty fight. Even steven. And we'll fight it out, we two, we shall. After all, I'm the part that *thinks!*" That was good, it was a triumph, he'd remember that. "Yes, by God, yes. I'm the part that thinks. If I didn't have you, even then I could still think!"

Instantly, he felt a pain strike his head. His cranium, crowding in slowly, began giving him some of his own treatment back.

At the end of the week he had postponed the Phoenix trip because of his health. Weighing himself on a penny scale he saw the slow glide of the red arrow as it pointed to: 164.

He groaned. "Why, I've weighed 175 for ten years. I can't have lost eleven pounds." He examined his cheeks in the fly-dotted mirror. Cold primitive fear rushed over him in odd little shivers. "Hold on! I know what you're about, *you.*"

He shook his finger at his bony face, particularly addressing his remarks to his superior maxillary, his inferior maxillary, to his cranium, and to his cervical vertebrae.

"You rum thing, you. Think you can starve me off, make me lose weight, eh? A victory for you, is that? Peel the flesh off, leave nothing but skin on bone. Trying to ditch me, so you can be supreme, eh? No, no!"

He fled into a cafeteria.

Ordering turkey, dressing, creamed potatoes, four vegetables, three desserts, he soon found he could not eat it, he was sick to his stomach. He forced himself. His teeth began to ache. "Bad teeth, is it?" he wanted to know, angrily. "I'll eat in spite of every tooth clanging and banging and rattling so they fall in my gravy."

His head ached, his breathing came hard from a constricted chest, his teeth pulsed with pain, but he had one small victory. He was about to drink milk when he stopped and poured it into a vase of nasturtiums. "No calcium for you, my boy, no more calcium for you. Never again shall I eat foods with calcium or other bone-fortifying minerals. I'll eat for one of us, not both, my lad."

"One hundred and fifty pounds," he said, the following week to his wife. "Do you see how I've changed?"

"For the better," said Clarisse. "You were always a little plump for your height, darling." She stroked his chin. "I like your face, it's so much nicer, the lines of it are so firm and strong now."

"They're not *my* lines, they're his, damn him! You mean to say you like him better than you like me?" he demanded indignantly.

"Him? Who's 'him'?"

In the parlor mirror, beyond Clarisse, his skull smiled back at him behind his fleshy grimace of hatred and despair.

Fuming, he popped malt tablets into his mouth. This was one way of gaining weight when you couldn't keep other foods down. Clarisse noticed the malt pellets. "But, darling, really, you don't have to gain the weight for me," she said.

Oh, shut up! he felt like saying.

She came to him and sat down and made him lie so his head was in her lap. "Darling," she said. "I've watched you lately. You're so—badly off. You don't say anything, but you look—hunted. You toss in bed at night. Maybe you should go to a psychiatrist. But I think I can tell you everything he would say. I've put it all together, from hints you've let escape you. I can tell you that you and your skeleton are one and the same, one nation, indivisible, with liberty and justice for all. United you stand, divided you fall. If you two fellows can't get along like an old married couple in the future, go back and see Dr. Burleigh. But, *first,* relax. You're in a vicious circle, the more you worry, the more your bones stick out, the more your bones stick out, the more you worry. After all, now, who picked this fight—you or that anonymous entity you claim is lurking around behind your alimentary canal?"

He closed his eyes. "I did. I guess I did. Oh, my darling, I love you so."

"You rest now," she said softly. "Rest and forget."

Mr. Harris felt buoyed up for half a day, then he began to sag again. It was all very well to say everything was imagination, but this particular skeleton, by God, was fighting back.

Harris set out for M. Munigant's office late in the day. Walking for half an hour until he found the address, he caught sight of the name M. Munigant initialed in ancient, flaking gold on a glass plate outside the building. Then, his bones seemed to explode from their moorings, blasted and erupting with pain. He could hardly see with his wet, pain-filled eyes. So violent were the pains that he staggered away. When he opened his eyes again, he had rounded a corner. M. Munigant's office was out of sight.

The pains ceased.

M. Munigant was the man to help him. He *must* be! If the sight of his gilt-lettered name could cause so titanic a reaction in the deepness of Harris's body, why, of course M. Munigant *must* be just the man.

But not today. Each time he tried to return to that office, the terrible pains laid him low. Perspiring, he had to give up, and stagger into a cocktail bar for respite.

Moving across the dim room of the cocktail lounge, he wondered briefly if a lot of blame couldn't be put on M. Munigant's shoulders; after all, it was Munigant who'd first drawn such specific attention to his skeleton, and brought home the entire psychological impact of it! Could M. Munigant be using him for some nefarious purpose? But what purpose? Silly to even suspect him. Just a little doctor. Trying to be helpful. Munigant and his jar of breadsticks. Ridiculous. M. Munigant was okay, okay.

There was a sight within the cocktail lounge to give him hope. A large fat man, round as a butterball, stood drinking consecutive beers at the bar. Now *there* was a successful man. Harris repressed a desire to go up, clap the fat man's shoulder, and inquire as to how he'd gone about impounding his bones. Yes, the fat man's skeleton was luxuriously closeted. There were pillows of

22

fat here, resilient bulges of it there, with several round chandeliers of fat under his chin. The poor skeleton was lost, it could never fight clear of *that* blubber; it may have tried once—but now, overwhelmed, not a bony echo of the fat man's supporter remained.

Not without envy, Harris approached the fat man as one might cut across the bow of an ocean liner. Harris ordered a drink, drank it, and then dared to address the fat man: "Glands?"

"You talking to me?" asked the fat man.

"Or is there a special diet?" wondered Harris. "I beg your pardon, but, as you see, I'm down. Can't seem to put on any weight. I'd like a stomach like that one of yours. Did you grow it because you were afraid of something?"

"You," announced the fat man, "are drunk. But—I *like* drunkards." He ordered more drinks. "Listen close. I'll tell you—

"Layer by layer," said the fat man, "twenty years, man and boy, I built this." He held his vast stomach like a globe of the world, teaching his audience its gastronomical geography. "It was no overnight circus. The tent was not raised before dawn on the wonders installed within. I have cultivated my inner organs as if they were thoroughbred dogs, cats, and other animals. My stomach is a fat pink Persian tom slumbering, rousing at intervals to purr, mew, growl, and cry for chocolate tit-bits. I feed it well, it will almost sit up for me. And, my dear fellow, my intestines are the rarest pure-bred Indian anacondas you ever viewed in the sleekest, coiled, fine, and ruddy health. Keep 'em in prime, I do, all my pets. For fear of something? Perhaps."

This called for another drink for both of them.

"Gain weight?" The fat man savored the words on his tongue. "Here's what you do; get yourself a quarreling bird of a wife, a baker's dozen of relatives who can flush a covey of troubles out from behind the veriest molehill. Add to these a sprinkling of business associates whose prime motivation is snatching your last lonely quid, and you are well on your way to getting fat. How so? In no time you'll begin subconsciously building fat betwixt yourself and them. A buffer epidermal state, a cellular wall. You'll soon find that eating is the only fun on earth. But one needs to be bothered by outside sources. Too many people in this world haven't enough to worry about, then they begin picking on *themselves*, and they lose weight. Meet all of the vile, terrible people you can possibly meet, and pretty soon you'll be adding the good old fat!"

And with that advice, the fat man launched himself out into the dark tide of night, swaying mightily and wheezing.

"That's exactly what Dr. Burleigh told me, slightly changed." said Harris thoughtfully. "Perhaps that trip to Phoenix, now, at this time—"

The trip from Los Angeles to Phoenix was a sweltering one, crossing, as it did, the desert on a broiling yellow day. Traffic was thin and inconstant, and for long stretches there would not be a car on the road for miles ahead or behind. Harris twitched his fingers on the steering wheel. Whether or not Creldon, in Phoenix, lent him the money he needed to start his business, it was still a good thing to get away, to put distance behind.

The car moved in the hot sluice of desert wind. The one Mr. H sat inside the other Mr. H. Perhaps both perspired. Perhaps both were miserable.

On a curve, the inside Mr. H suddenly constricted the outer flesh, causing him to jerk forward on the hot steering wheel.

The car plunged off the road into deepest sand. It half turned over.

Night came on, a wind rose, the road was lonely and silent with little traffic. Those few cars that passed went swiftly on their way, their view obstructed. Mr. Harris lay unconscious until, very late, he heard a wind rising out of the desert, felt the sting of little sand needles on his cheeks, and opened his eyes.

Morning found him gritty-eyed and wandering in thoughtless, senseless circles, having, in his delirium, gotten away from the road. At noon he sprawled in the poor shade of a bush. The sun struck into him with a keen sword edge, cutting through to his—bones. A vulture circled.

Harris's parched lips cracked open, weakly. "So that's it?" he whimpered, red-eyed, bristle-cheeked. "One way or another you'll wreck me, walk me, starve me, thirst me, kill me." He swallowed dry burrs of dust. "Sun cooks off my flesh so you can peek forth. Vultures lunch and breakfast from me, and then there you'll lie, grinning. Grinning with victory. Like a bleached xylophone strewn and played by vultures with an ear for odd music. You'd like that. Freedom."

He walked on through a landscape that shivered and bubbled in the direct pour of sunlight; stumbling, falling flat, lying down to feed himself little mouths of flame. The air was blue alcohol flame, and vultures roasted and steamed and glittered as they flew in glides and circles. Phoenix. The road. Car. Water. Safety.

"Hey!"

Somebody called from way off in the blue alcohol flame.

Mr. Harris propped himself up.

"Hey!"

The call was repeated. A crunching of footsteps, quick.

With a cry of unbelievable relief, Harris rose, only to collapse again, into the arms of someone in a uniform with a badge. . . .

The car tediously hauled, repaired, Phoenix reached, Harris found himself in such an unholy state of mind that the business transaction was more a numb pantomime than anything else. Even when he got the loan and held the money in his hand, it meant nothing. This Thing within him like a hard white sword in a scabbard tainted his business, his eating, colored his love for Clarisse, made it unsafe to trust an automobile; all in all this Thing had to be put in its place before he could have love for business or anything. That desert incident had brushed too closely. Too near the bone, one might say with an ironic twist of one's mouth. Harris heard himself thanking Mr. Creldon, dimly, for the money. Then he turned his car and motored back across the long miles, this time cutting across to San Diego, so that he would miss that desert stretch between El Centro and Beaumont. He drove north along the coast. He didn't trust that desert. But—careful! Salt waves boomed, hissing on the beach outside Laguna. Sand, fish, and crustacea would cleanse his bones as swiftly as vultures. Slow down on the curves over the surf.

If anything happened, he wanted cremation. The two of them'd burn together that way. None of this graveyard burial stuff where little crawling things eat and leave nothing but unmantled bone! No, they'd burn. Damn him! He was sick. Where could he turn? Clarisse? Burleigh? Munigant? Bone specialist. Munigant. Well?

"Darling!" trilled Clarisse, kissing him, so he winced at the solidness of her teeth and jaw behind the passionate exchange.

"Darling," he said, slowly wiping his lips with his wrist, trembling.

"You look thinner; oh, darling, the business deal—?"

"It went through. Yeah, it went through. I guess. Yeah, it did," he said.

She enthused. She kissed him again. Lord, he couldn't even enjoy kisses anymore because of this obsession. They ate a slow, falsely cheerful dinner, with Clarisse laughing and encouraging him. He studied the phone, several times he picked it up indecisively, then laid it down. His wife walked in, putting on her coat and hat. "Well, sorry, but I have to leave now," she laughed, and pinched him lightly on the cheek. "Come on now, cheer up! I'll be back from Red Cross in three hours. You lie around and snooze. I simply *have* to go."

When Clarisse was gone, Harris dialed the number, nervously. "M. Munigant?"

The explosions and the sickness in his body after he set the phone down were unbelievable. His bones were racked with every kind of pain, cold and hot, he had ever thought of or experienced in wildest nightmare. He swallowed all the aspirin he could find in an effort to stave off the assault; but when the

26

doorbell finally rang an hour later, he could not move, he lay weak and exhausted, panting, tears streaming down his cheeks, like a man on a torture rack. Would M. Munigant go away if the door was not answered?

"Come in!" he tried to gasp it out. "Come in, for God's sake!" M. Munigant came in. Thank God the door had been unlocked.

Oh, but Mr. Harris looked terrible. M. Munigant stood in the center of the living room, small and dark. Harris nodded at him. The pains rushed through him, hitting him with large iron hammers and hooks. M. Munigant's eyes glittered as he saw Harris's protuberant bones. Ah, he saw that Mr. Harris was now psychologically prepared for aid. Was it not so? Harris nodded again, feebly, sobbing. M. Munigant still whistled when he talked; something odd about his tongue and the whistling. No matter. Through his shimmering eyes, Harris seemed to see M. Munigant shrink, get smaller. Imagination, of course. Harris sobbed out his story of the Phoenix trip. M. Munigant sympathized. This skeleton was a—a traitor! They would *fix* him for once and for all! "M. Munigant," sighed Harris, faintly. "I—I never noticed before. You have such an odd, odd tongue. Round. Tubelike. Hollow? Guess it's my eyes. Don't mind me. Delirious. I'm ready. What do I do?"

M. Munigant whistled softly, appreciatively, coming closer. If Mr. Harris would relax in his chair, and open his mouth? The lights were switched off. M. Munigant peered into Harris's dropped jaw. Wider, please. It had been so hard, that first visit, to help Harris, with both body and bone in rebellion. Now, he had cooperation from the flesh of the man, anyway, even if the skeleton was acting up somewhat. In the darkness, M. Munigant's voice got small, small, tiny, tiny. The whistling became high and shrill. Now. Relax, Mr. Harris. *Now!*

Harris felt his jaws pressed violently in all directions, his tongue depressed as with a spoon, his throat clogged. He gasped for breath. Whistle. He couldn't breathe! He was corked. Something squirmed, cork-screwed his cheeks out, bursting his jaws.

Like a hot-water douche, something squirted into his sinuses, his ears clanged! "Ahhh!" shrieked Harris, gagging. His head, its carapaces riven, shattered, hung loose. Agony shot into his lungs, around.

Harris could breathe again, momentarily. His watery eyes sprang wide. He shouted. His ribs, like sticks picked up and bundled, were loosened in him. Pain! He fell to the floor, rocking, rolling, wheezing out his hot breath.

Light flickered in his senseless eyeballs; he felt his senseless eyeballs, he felt his limbs swiftly cast loose and free, expertly. Through streaming eyes, he saw the parlor.

The room was empty.

M. Munigant was gone.

"Help!"

Then he heard it.

Deep down in the subterranean fissures of his bodily well, he heard the minute, unbelievable noises; little smackings and twistings and little dry chippings and grindings and nuzzling sounds—like a tiny hungry mouse down in the red-blooded dimness, gnawing ever so earnestly and expertly at what may have been, but was not, a submerged timber!

Clarisse, walking along the sidewalk, held her head high and marched straight toward her house on Saint James Place. She was thinking of the Red Cross and a thousand other things as she turned the corner and almost ran into this little dark man who smelled of iodine.

Clarisse would have ignored him if it were not for the fact that as she passed he took something long, white and oddly familiar from his coat and proceeded to chew on it as if it were a peppermint stick. Its end devoured, his extraordinary tongue darted within the white confection, sucking out the filling, making contented noises. He was still crunching his goody as she proceeded up the sidewalk to her house, turned the doorknob and walked in.

"Darling?" she called, smiling around. "Darling, where are you?"

She shut the door, walked down the hall and into the living room.

"Darling . . ."

She stared at the floor for twenty seconds, trying to understand.

She screamed.

Outside in the sycamore darkness, the little man pierced a long white stick with intermittent holes; then softly, sighing, lips puckered, played a little sad tune upon the improvised instrument to accompany the shrill and awful singing of Clarisse's voice as she stood in the living room.

Many times as a little girl, Clarisse had run on the beach sands, stepped on a jellyfish and screamed. It was not so bad, finding an intact, gelatin-skinned jellyfish in one's living room. One could step back from it.

It was when the jellyfish *called you by name* . . .

BRONZE

W. M. TIDMARSH

At the auction viewing it was lying on the central table where the better class bric-a-brac was displayed and it stood out by its incongruity. Among the plate and china, the cut glass, the tureen and pewter stood this squat, dull-colored object: a bronze model of some sort of dragonlike animal. The body was a slightly elongated sphere about ten inches long, the curved tail extended for about three more, and the broad, flattened head at the other end brought the overall length to about fifteen inches. The body was elaborately scaled and covered all over with small, raised flowerlike pustules which gave it a somewhat decaying appearance. The face was deceptive. Looked at from above, as it stood on the table, it looked genial, avuncular even, with wide-spaced eyes, round holes in the metal that looked as if they were backed by black velvet, a snub nose and a heavy walrus moustache. The beast seemed to look merrily, slyly, up at me.

But then I lifted it and as I brought the surprisingly heavy model to eye level the look on the face changed. Below the moustache gaped a broad mouth, turned down fiercely at the corners where the moustache followed the line of the mouth in a menacing way, between the serrated rows of teeth the tongue, green with verdigris unlike the rest of the model, seemed to hover. At this angle it looked altogether more lifelike and sinister.

I put down the bronze, my curiosity satisfied and chastened, and then caught sight of Frank Rolands. Frank has a more catholic taste than I and this was just the sort of thing that might take his fancy. I called him over: "Here's something in your line I should think, just about ugly enough to feel at home in your clutter."

He picked the model up and examined it: "I must say, it is rather fine," he said, "though I'm damned if I know where it comes from. I bet, though, that it's not as old as it looks. I expect it was made last month in Hong Kong and there's one like it in every auction in the country just now."

Nevertheless, at the sale next day he bought it. We had a drink afterwards and Frank pulled his bronze prize out of a paper bag and put it on the pub table. It seemed to me less plump and jolly looking than it had on the previous day. But I put this down to the different setting and light. As he sat there examining it, Frank put his finger, the second finger of his right hand to be precise, into the beast's mouth and rubbed the green tongue. I recall watching him do it with a slight feeling of revulsion.

"If it's as new as you say how did they get that verdigris on the tongue? I thought that took years of weathering to develop," I said. Frank didn't answer. Instead he took out his handkerchief and wiped his finger vigorously.

"That was odd," he said. "D'you know it felt just as if that thing's tongue licked me; it had that warm, roughish feeling of a dog's tongue and its edges seemed to curl around my finger."

I laughed, "It's grateful to you for giving it a home, I expect."

"No, really, I could have sworn I'd been licked. My finger didn't look wet yet it felt slimy. Anyway," he went on cheerily, "as you say, if it licks me at least it likes me."

Frank and I both had rooms in college and usually saw each other fairly frequently but it was almost a week before I met him again. I called in to return a book and at once noticed the bronze beast squatting on its short legs with their webbed and clawed feet on a low bookcase near the window. Again, from this angle, it had the mischievous, friendly look that I had first noticed. I saw that Frank's hand was bandaged. "What happened," I asked, "did Fido here get past the licking to the biting stage?" Frank laughed. "Don't you malign my beastie," he said, "d'you know I think I was wrong about his humble origins. I suspect that I may have got a bargain and that he may be a good piece."

"And the hand?" I asked.

"Oh, it's just a bit of a rash but I've got some greasy ointment on it so I keep it bandaged."

He went to make coffee and I looked more closely at the bronze. The scaly skin with its flock of pustules gave a strangely vivid impression of having just settled after shivering in that curious way that some animals have of rippling their skins; I could almost imagine that I had looked just as it came to rest. I did not pick it up this time but bent down to look from a different angle and again I was struck by the change in the expression on the face as it came level with my own. It became menacing; the mischievous look in the black eyes turned knowing and malevolent and the tongue seemed almost to flicker in the case of its mouth. It had a disturbing effect, that still yet lively gaze, and I quickly straightened up and was about to turn away altogether when I was struck by the impression that the stance of the bronze beast had changed since I had seen it a week before. In the pub it had seemed slightly leaner than when I had first seen it, now it looked more alert and I noticed its pointed ears for the first time. It wasn't a gross change and yet it was, or seemed, distinct, as though it had braced its rear legs a little more in readiness for a spring. But, I told myself, it was no doubt again a trick of the light or the angle. "A good piece or not, I'm afraid I find your beastie rather repulsive," I said to Frank when he returned with the coffee.

The following day Frank came around for a drink before lunch and not only his hand but his forearm was now bandaged. The rash was spreading, though his doctor was sure it was a simple infection of some kind and would soon respond to the treatment he had prescribed. It was a warm day and Frank was wearing a T-shirt: Between the sleeve and the top of the bandage, there was a gap and as we sat and talked I saw a brown mottled stain spreading above the dressing towards the elbow. Frank noticed it too, and tried to hide it with his hand.

"I think you ought to get a second opinion about that business," I said, and he withdrew his hand. "It seems to be spreading rather quickly, don't you think? Why don't you go down to see Joe Simpson at the hospital? He's bound to know a dermatologist." Simpson was a mutual friend in the medical faculty.

To my surprise, Frank agreed, and shortly afterwards left to look up Simpson. Early that evening Simpson rang me and asked whether I knew about the rash and suggested that I might look in on Frank as he had appeared rather depressed after leaving the hospital.

I went around to see Frank at once and he answered the door to me still in his T-shirt and with a towel draped over his now unbandaged arm.

"I hear you're not feeling too bright," I said, "so I've brought a bottle around—unless you prefer to go out?"

"No, I'd rather stay in, I think. Come on in and I'll get the glasses."

From the kitchen he called: "D'you want water or soda?"

"Water," I said, and once more found myself gazing at the bronze dragon. The evening shadows on the face gave it a mocking expression and now the eyes that had seemed so black before seemed paler than the bronze itself. But it was not this that held my attention but the impression that again the beast had changed its stance. Once more it was so slight a change as to defy certainty, but it seemed to have gone further back on its haunches and to be gathering itself to a tense posture. Frank called for me to open the bottle and it was easy enough, then, to persuade myself that, as before, it was the light and a faulty memory that were playing tricks.

Frank sat with his arm still covered by the towel and fairly gulped his Scotch.

"So, what did they say at the hospital?" I asked.

"Nothing very definite, though they seemed as interested as they were puzzled. Changed the treatment, and I have to go back tomorrow."

"Did they have any views about what caused it?"

"No," and he drained his glass.

"D'you have any ideas?"

"Not really," he said, and passed me his glass for a refill. "Oh, by the way, they're pretty sure it's not infectious or contagious." He was being evasive.

"So what is your idea about the cause?" I pressed.

He paused for a long while. "Well, it sounds bloody silly," he eventually began, "but I think it has something to do with touching that thing's tongue in the pub that day. You remember I had the curious impression of having been licked by it?" He stopped abruptly.

"Go on," I said. He drank again, but didn't continue.

"Did it start on that hand?"

"Yes, on that finger. It started as an itch. Not at once, the next day, in the evening and it has been spreading ever since. But it's ridiculous. I've scraped some traces of the verdigris off that tongue and analyzed it and chemically it is just the same as the verdigris on other bronzes that I handle regularly and they have no effect on me."

"You didn't mention this to the medics?" I asked.

"And have them think I've got a brain rash as well? You bet I didn't!"

I stood up to get the soda, and as I passed Frank I accidentally pulled the towel off his affected arm. Frank didn't move but he looked up at me. "You see what I mean?" he said.

I saw what he meant very clearly. The rash on his arm was not like any rash I had ever seen before. The skin had darkened and had changed texture, taking on a smooth, stretched, shiny appearance like the skin on a bald head. The fingers, palm, and wrist were already sprinkled with small blebs, not inflamed or infected, but standing out clearly and some were already beginning to show a formalized flowerlike design.

I glanced across at the bronze beast, but now it stood in deep shadow, for the daylight had faded and the light from the desk lamp did not reach there.

"I see what you mean, or at least I can guess," I said. "Look, Frank, I don't know anything about skin diseases at all, but I can see no reason to suppose that this isn't simply a rare infection. Have you thought that it might even be an allergy?" I said eagerly. "I'll bet that's what it is, an allergy! Have you handled anything unusual recently?" and immediately I had said it I saw that I had undermined my attempts at reassurance.

"Precisely," Frank said, "and you know what. I told you that that beast licked me, and it did you know! Oh, I know it sounds incredible, but it did."

"But I've handled it myself; I handled it before you, remember?"

"And did you put your finger in its mouth?"

"Well, no—but I'll go and do so now if it will reassure you," and repugnant though the idea was to me I stood up.

"For God's sake, don't!" Frank cried and leaped up himself. He sounded so alarmed that I sat down again.

"Oh, let's forget the whole bloody thing for tonight," he said, "and get tight—they can always cut the damned arm off, I suppose." So we sat and got drunk and forgot the bronze beast and the bronzing arm.

Next day I slept in and didn't see Frank until he returned from his visit to the hospital. All they had done, it seemed, was to do more tests, but they had offered no further diagnosis or treatment. By now the rash had covered one shoulder and was moving

36

across his back and chest; it was even beginning, I noticed, to be visible above the polo-necked sweater he wore. Frank uncovered his hand to show me. The skin was dark coppery brown, the pustules clearly defined. The hand looked as though it had been dipped into metallic paint. I must have gasped at the sight, and Frank said, "It begins to feel like metal, too, as though my hand was wrapped in foil." He tapped it with a pencil and it made a dull sound. "Tomorrow," he said, "it will ring like that damned bronze and it will get harder and harder and I shall be trapped inside." He began to shake and turned away so that I should not see his face.

"Why don't you get rid of the thing? Sell it, throw it away, destroy it?" I said.

"No! No, not yet," he said harshly, actually moving to put himself between me and the bronze. "If it is connected with this business, it may be important to have it around."

A few minutes later I left Frank and went to the auctioneers. I wanted to know where the bronze had come from, who had sent it in for sale. It turned out to be part of a whole consignment of objects from the estate of a man who had recently died. I got hold of the name of the solicitor who had acted as executor and was lucky enough to catch him as his last client of the day left. I explained my presence and in particular my interest in the bronze dragon that had belonged to his late client, Sir Paul Torrance.

"As a matter of fact," he said, "I remember it well. I had dinner with him not long after he came back from the East, where he bought it. I was examining it, can't say I liked it much by the way, when my signet ring (I have a bad habit of playing with it rather than wearing it) slipped into its mouth and I had the deuce of a job poking it free, it seemed to get caught somewhere under the tongue."

"D'you know where he happened to buy it?" I asked.

"Actually, it was the last thing he did buy and he got it . . . let me see," he reached for a box file, "in Djakarta. There's no receipt here, only a note written in his own hand and saying how much he

paid, but not from whom he bought it; simply says 'got it surprisingly cheap from a chap who seemed most anxious to sell,
probably stolen.' "

"Was he in Djakarta himself or did he buy it through an agent,
d'you know?" I asked.

"Oh, he was there himself and from this note it seems he
bought it himself. Actually, it was there that he probably caught
the trouble that more or less led to his death."

"What was that?" I asked. "I seem to recall reading a report of
his death, but no details."

"It's a rather strange story and the full details weren't made
public. He'd gone to a clinic in Lucerne to get treatment for a skin
disease he'd developed, the thing he'd picked up out East, and he
was drowned in the lake while he was there—that's what I meant
when I said the infection led indirectly to his death."

"You said the full details weren't published. Was there some
foul play or something?"

"No, not really. In fact, it rather looked as if he might have
done it deliberately himself. Someone saw him fall into the water
from the boat he'd hired, and when he didn't reappear, this chap
phoned the police. They searched the lake, found nothing, and
decided to wait for the body to float. But it didn't, so they
searched again and they found it lying on the bottom, not trapped
or anything, just lying there. Most extraordinary thing. There
were no weights attached to it and yet it didn't float, and it was so
heavy they had a job raising it. Anyway, as I say, the whole thing
was handled very well and an accidental death verdict was
brought in."

I thanked him and left and I recall feeling suddenly very cold as
I stepped into the still warm air and I realized that my whole body
was soaked in sweat. I didn't call on Frank straight away but went
to my own rooms to think. I called on him later, but he was out
and I did not try to see him again that day. I called on him the
following day before lunch and at first got no answer to my ring. I
rang again and from behind the door he asked who it was. When I

told him, he opened the door, and by the time I had got in he had turned away and walked back into his study, where he stood looking out of the window.

"How are you, Frank? Any response to the new treatment yet?" He didn't speak, but turned around to face me. The strong light was behind him and at first I could not clearly see his features. Then I saw that the lower part of his face, up to the cheekbones, had deepened in color and was sprinkled, though more sparsely than elsewhere on his body, with darker blebs. He let me look for a moment then covered his lower face with a towel he had around his shoulders.

"Come and sit down," I said, "and do, please, remove that towel unless it is part of the treatment." Still without speaking he sat down opposite me and lowered the towel, and I saw then that tears were streaming from his eyes.

"What did they say at the hospital?" I asked.

"They suggested that I should go in so that they could do more tests." He half smiled, but there was a mocking hopelessness in his eyes that was the most distressing look I had ever seen.

"You'll go in, of course, Frank," I said, "you've nothing possible to lose by it."

"Nor to gain, I suspect," he said. "This isn't something that medicine can cure—and I think you know that as well as I do. I simply can't understand how I came to be a victim of whatever it is."

After what I had learned the previous day, I was by now convinced that it was only the owner of the bronze that was at risk from whatever evil was in it. I did not tell Frank what I had discovered about the model's origin as it could do nothing to relieve his distress or delay the complete despair that I feared was approaching.

"Look, Frank, why don't you destroy the bronze, or throw it away, or get rid of it anyway? Once it's no longer in your possession, I'm sure you will be rid of whatever thing you have got. Please Frank, let me take it away and smash it."

At this he sprang up and almost screamed his answer: "No, don't touch it. While I still have it, there may be a chance for me." His look had changed from one of despair to one of ferocity and I was reminded then of his remark about a rash on his brain.

"Well, let's have a drink then," I said weakly, "I'm sure you could do with one and I certainly could."

He calmed down at this suggestion and fetched the whisky. We were neither of us heavy lunchtime drinkers, but while I sipped my drink Frank again drank quickly and refilled several times. It occurred to me that he might already have been drinking that morning, which would have accounted for his unusual behavior, and this seemed all the more likely when he began to drop off to sleep in his chair. In a short while he was sound asleep and I noticed that already, during the short time I had been with him, the dark stain had begun to encroach on his temples and his forehead.

I really do not know now whether I would have taken the bronze beast and destroyed it while Frank slept, but I suppose I had intended to, for it seemed to be his only chance of survival. Anyway, once he was sound asleep I went across to the bookcase and seized the hideous model. Immediately there was a most terrible roar from my sleeping friend, and he awoke clutching his sides and screaming and gasping with pain. At once I put the bronze down and went across to him, and as I reached his chair he collapsed onto the floor.

He appeared to have fainted, but as I raised his shoulders he came to and half shook himself. "My God," he said, "what happened? I thought I was going to die with the pain, my ribs were being crushed. I couldn't breathe."

"I think it was probably a cramp or a spasm brought on by the way you were sitting," I said, and thanked God that he seemed to accept this explanation. I poured him another glass of whisky and while he still had it in his hand induced him to go and lie on his bed and rest. We half staggered to the bedroom and the terrible beast seemed to grin at us as we passed.

I left him and went back to my own rooms and was physically sick. When I had recovered, I rang Joe Simpson at the hospital and told him about the attack Frank had suffered, though without telling him the circumstances—I had decided to tell him those once Frank was safely in hospital. He agreed to arrange for Frank's admission that evening. I had a few things to do and thought it would be better to let Frank sleep as long as possible, so I did not go to see him again until later that afternoon. I called to him through the mail slot and he let me in. The rash had completely covered his face by now and the pustules were beginning to take on their characteristic flowerlike form, yet he seemed rather brighter and his eyes were less hopeless. I explained that he could go into hospital that evening under Joe's personal care and he agreed to go.

"But first," he said, "I want to do one other thing. Whether I am right or wrong about the cause of this horrible business, and I know that you, too, think that I am right, it is a mysterious affair. You know that I've never had any time, as a scientist, for magic or voodoo or that sort of thing, but I am going to talk to D——," (and he mentioned the name of a well-known authority on the occult who lived in the area). "I've telephoned for an appointment and he'll see me this afternoon. I'm going to drive over now. And after that I'm in your hands."

By 7:30 P.M. Frank had not returned and as I was anxious to get him into hospital that evening I rang D—— myself. He confirmed that Frank had had an appointment but he had not kept it. I didn't know what to do. At first I thought of contacting the police but that seemed premature, so I set off myself for the village where D—— lived. I reasoned that it was possible that Frank had broken down and felt unable to seek help with his disfigured face. About halfway there, on a straight stretch of road, I saw the flashing orange and blue lights of the breakdown and police vehicles, and I stopped just beyond the smashed and burned-out wreck they were trying to retrieve. I walked back and spoke to the police driver.

41

"We're not even sure of what make of car it is yet, let alone who it belongs to," he said. "Nothing else seemed to have been involved, it left the road, smashed into that tree, and then caught fire."

"There was someone in it. You're sure?" I asked.

"There was a body in it, or at least the charred bits of a body, but we don't even know what sex it was yet, let alone its identity."

"You've no idea who's the owner of the car?"

"The only thing we have is the last letter and last number of the registration number, *E* and 6—but I expect we'll have to ring in, sir." But *E* and 6 were details enough. I knew Frank's registration number as well as my own.

I don't recall the drive home, but when I got in I phoned Joe Simpson and told him what had happened. I must have broken down on the phone as he came around a short while later and gave me a sedative. It was another couple of days before I felt able to function again. By this time the remains in the car had been identified as those of Frank and I became aware of a consequence of his death which temporarily replaced grief with terror.

Frank and I had gone from being colleagues to being friends, and we had grown progressively closer as time went on. Part of the basis of our friendship had been our shared, though different, interest in collecting, and we had each said from time to time that each would leave the other his collection in his will. In fact, I had not yet done this, it had hardly seemed necessary, but I suspected that Frank, who was a very meticulous person, probably had, so the day after his funeral I went around to see his solicitor, who happened also to be mine and a friend. The will had not yet been proved and strictly speaking I suppose I should not have asked, but he confirmed that Frank had left me his entire collection.

"Did he specify items, I mean, would the latest things he acquired have been included?" I asked.

"He didn't need to specify, he simply said all the items, the receipts for which would be found in a specific file, were to be considered his collection." The bill for the bronze would, I was sure, have been in the file.

"But," I said, "until the will is read they aren't, strictly speaking, mine—I mean, I don't actually own any of them, do I?"

"No, but that's a strange question, surely," he said and looked puzzled and shocked.

I apologized without explaining and left him. I felt sure that whatever dreadful power that bronze beast had was only directed at its owner. That was why handling it hadn't affected me or Sir Paul Torrance's solicitor, even though he had put his fingers in its mouth. And I was, unavoidably, to be the next owner.

I had a key to Frank's rooms and now, wearing gloves and carrying an armful of newspapers and a plastic box, I let myself in. The bronze dragon stood where I had last seen it and when I got close it looked as when I had first seen it. It squatted plumply square on all four stubby legs with no suggestion of being poised to pounce or lunge. The broad face seemed from above to have a wistful grin on it, the heavy moustache drooped in a gentle, comic way. I did not bend down to look at it head on, I did not lift it to eye level, I simply wrapped it in newspaper and stuffed it in the box.

I had hoped to hire a boat and drop the bronze into deep water some way off shore, but there were no boats available when I reached Marbeach. I walked with the box up on to the low cliffs and when I came to a place that looked directly down into what seemed a deep pool I took out the bronze beast and, still wearing gloves and without looking at it again I threw it down and out into the water.

The ripples settled on the still sea-pool and then the late sun broke through the haze and, apparently reflected off the white cliff-face below me, shone into the pool and I could see the bottom strewn with rocks and colored stones and swaths of seaweed. There among them lay the beast. As I watched I thought I saw the short legs move and the webbed feet begin to paddle slowly and deliberately, and it seemed that the plump and mottled body quivered and the black eyes raised themselves towards me. But then the light faded and ripples fretted the surface once more. I stood for one moment longer and then hurried away.

I have thought this morning of going back to retrieve it—there is still time, for the will has not yet been read—and taking it far out to sea to be rid of it, or casting it into a furnace, or smashing it to pieces with a hammer. But what if I go back and it is not there? And I know it will not be there, but I do not know where it is. Yet. But tomorrow I become its owner.

AS IS

ROBERT SILVERBERG

"As is," the auto dealer said, jamming his thumbs under his belt. "Two hundred fifty bucks and drive it away. I'm not pretending it's perfect, but I got to tell you, you're getting a damned good hunk of car for the price."

"As is," Sam Norton said.

"As is. Strictly as is."

Norton looked a little doubtful. "Maybe she drives well, but with a trunk that doesn't open—"

"So what?" the dealer snorted. "You told me yourself you're renting a U-Haul to get your stuff to California. What do you need a trunk for? Look, when you get out to the Coast and have a little time, take the car to a garage, tell 'em the story, and maybe five minutes with a blowtorch—"

"Why didn't you do that while you had the car in stock?"

The dealer looked evasive. "We don't have time to fool with details like that."

Norton let the point pass. He walked around the car again,

giving it a close look from all angles. It was a smallish dark green four-door sedan, with the finish and trim in good condition, a decent set of tires, and a general glow that comes only when a car has been well cared for. The upholstery was respectable, the radio was in working order, the engine was—as far as he could judge—okay, and a test drive had been smooth and easy. The car seemed to be a reasonably late model, too; it had shoulder-harness safety belts and emergency blinkers.

There was only one small thing wrong with it. The trunk didn't open. It wasn't just a case of a jammed lock, either; somebody had fixed this car so the trunk *couldn't* open. With great care the previous owner had apparently welded the trunk shut; nothing was visible back there except a dim line to mark the place where the lid might once have lifted.

What the hell, though. The car was otherwise in fine shape, and he wasn't in a position to be too picky. Overnight, practically, they had transferred him to the Los Angeles office, which was fine in terms of getting out of New York in the middle of a lousy winter, but not so good as far as his immediate finances went. The company didn't pay moving costs, only transportation; he had been handed four one-way tourist-class tickets, and that was that. So he had put Ellen and the kids aboard the first jet to L.A., cashing in his own ticket so he could use the money for the moving job. He figured to do it the slow but cheap way: rent a U-Haul trailer, stuff the family belongings into it, and set out via turnpike for California, hoping that Ellen would have found an apartment by the time he got there. Only he couldn't trust his present clunker of a car to get him very far west of Parsippany, New Jersey, let alone through the Mojave Desert. So here he was, trying to pick up an honest used job for about five hundred bucks, which was all he could afford to lay out on the spot.

And here was the man at the used-car place offering him this very attractive vehicle—with its single peculiar defect—for only two and a half bills, which would leave him with that much extra cash cushion for the expenses of his transcontinental journey.

And he didn't *really* need a trunk, driving alone. He could keep his suitcase on the back seat and stash everything else in the U-Haul. And it shouldn't be all that hard to have some mechanic in L.A. cut the trunk open for him and get it working again. On the other hand, Ellen was likely to chew him out for having bought a car that was sealed up that way; she had let him have it before on other "bargains" of that sort. On the third hand, the mystery of the sealed trunk appealed to him. Who knew what he'd find in there once he opened it up? Maybe the car had belonged to a smuggler who had had to hide a hot cargo fast, and the trunk was full of lovely golden ingots, diamonds, or ninety-year-old cognac, which the smuggler had planned to reclaim a few weeks later, except that something had come up. On the fourth hand—

The dealer said, "How'd you like to take her out for another test spin, then?"

Norton shook his head. "Don't think I need to. I've got a good idea of how she rides."

"Well, then let's step into the office and close the deal."

Sidestepping the maneuver, Norton said, "What year did you say she was?"

"Oh, about a '64, '65."

"You aren't sure?"

"You can't really tell with these foreign jobs sometimes. You know, they don't change the model for five, six, ten years in a row, except in little ways that only an expert would notice. Take Volkswagen, for instance—'

"And I just realized," Norton cut in, "that you never told me what make she is, either."

"Peugeot, maybe, or some kind of Fiat," said the dealer hazily. "One of those kind."

"You don't *know*?"

A shrug. "Well, we checked a lot of the style books going back a few years, but there are so damn many of these foreign cars around, and some of them they import only a few thousand, and well— So we couldn't figure it out."

Norton wondered how he was going to get spare parts for a car of unknown make and uncertain date. Then he realized that he was thinking of the car as his already, even though the more he considered the deal, the less he liked it. And then he thought of those ingots in the trunk. The rare cognac. The suitcase full of diamonds.

He said, "Shouldn't the registration say something about the year and make?"

The dealer shifted his weight from foot to foot. "Matter of fact, we don't have the registration. But it's perfectly legitimate. Hey, look, I'd like to get this car out of my lot, so maybe we'll call it two twenty-five, huh?"

"It all sounds pretty mysterious. Where'd you get the car, anyway?"

"There was this little guy who brought it in, about a year ago, a year ago last November, I think it was. Give it a valve job, he said. I'll be back in a month—got to take a sudden business trip. Paid in advance for the tune-up and a month's storage and everything. Wouldn't you know that was the last we ever saw of him? Well, we stored his damn car here free for over a year, but that's it, now we got to get it out of the place. The lawyer says we can take possession for the storage charge."

"If I buy it, you'll give me a paper saying you had the right to sell it?"

"Sure. Sure."

"And what about getting the registration? Shifting the insurance over from my old heap? All the red tape?"

"I'll handle everything," the dealer said. "Just you take the car outa here."

"Two hundred," Norton said. "As is."

The dealer sighed. "It's a deal. As is."

A light snow was falling when Norton began his cross-country hegira three days later. It was an omen, but he was not sure what kind; he decided that the snow was intended as his last view of a dreary winter phenomenon he wouldn't be seeing again, for a while. According to the *Times,* yesterday's temperature range in L.A. had been 66 low, 79 high. Not bad for January.

He slouched down behind the wheel, let his foot rest lightly on the accelerator, and sped westward at a sane, sensible 45 miles per hour. That was about as fast as he dared go with the bulky U-Haul trailing behind. He hadn't had much experience driving with a trailer—he was a computer salesman, and computer salesmen don't carry sample computers—but he got the hang of it pretty fast. You just had to remember that your vehicle was now a segmented organism, and make your turns accordingly. God bless turnpikes, anyhow. Just drive on, straight and straight and straight, heading toward the land of the sunset with only a few gentle curves and half a dozen traffic lights along the way.

The snow thickened some. But the car responded beautifully, hugging the road, and the windshield wipers kept his view clear. He hadn't expected to buy a foreign car for the trip at all; when he had set out, it was to get a good solid Plymouth or Chevy, something heavy and sturdy to take him through the wide open spaces. But he had no regrets about this smaller car. It had all the power and pickup he needed, and with that trailer bouncing along behind him he wouldn't have much use for all that extra horsepower, anyway.

He was in a cheerful, relaxed mood. The car seemed comforting and protective, a warm enclosing environment that would contain and shelter him through the thousands of miles ahead. He was still close enough to New York to be able to get Mozart on the radio, which was nice. The car's heater worked well. There wasn't much traffic. The snow itself, new and white and fluffy, was all the more beautiful for the knowledge that he was leaving it behind. He even enjoyed the solitude. It would be restful, in a way, driving on and on through Ohio and Kansas and Colorado or Arizona or whatever states lay between him and Los Angeles.

Five or six days of peace and quiet, no need to make small talk, no kids to amuse. . . .

His frame of mind began to darken not long after he got on the Pennsylvania Turnpike. If you have enough time to think, you will eventually think of the things you should have thought of before; and now, as he rolled through the thickening snow on this gray and silent afternoon, certain aspects of a trunkless car occurred to him that in his rush to get on the road he had succeeded in overlooking earlier. What about a tool kit, for instance? If he had a flat, what would he use for a jack and a wrench? That led him to a much more chilling thought: What would he use for a spare tire? A trunk was something more than a cavity back of the rear seat; in most cars it contained highly useful objects.

None of which he had with him.

None of which he had even thought about until just this minute.

He contemplated the prospects of driving from coast to coast without a spare tire and without tools, and his mood of warm security evaporated abruptly. At the next exit, he decided, he'd hunt for a service station and pick up a tire, fast. There would be room for it on the back seat next to his luggage. And while he was at it, he might as well buy—

The U-Haul, he suddenly observed, was jackknifing around awkwardly in back, as though its wheels had just lost traction. A moment later the car was doing the same, and he found himself moving laterally in a beautiful skid across an unsanded slick patch on the highway. Steer in the direction of the skid, that's what you're supposed to do, he told himself, strangely calm. Somehow he managed to keep his foot off the brake despite all natural inclinations, and watched in quiet horror as car and trailer slid placidly across the empty lane to his right and came to rest, upright and facing forward, in the piled-up snowbank along the shoulder of the road.

He let out his breath slowly, scratched his chin, and gently fed the car some gas. The spinning wheels made a high-pitched whining sound against the snow. He went nowhere. He was stuck.

The little man had a ruddy-cheeked face, white hair so long it curled at the ends, and metal-rimmed spectacles. He glanced at the snow-covered autos in the used-car lot, scowled, and trudged towards the showroom.

"Came to pick up my car," he announced. "Valve job. Delayed by business in another part of the world."

The dealer looked uncomfortable. "The car's not here."

"So I see. Get it, then."

"We more or less sold it several days ago."

"*Sold it?* Sold my car? *My car?*"

"Which you abandoned. Which we stored here for over a year. This ain't no parking lot here. Look, I talked to my lawyer first, and he said—"

"All right. All right. Who was the purchaser?"

"A guy, he was transferred to California and had to get a car fast to drive out. He—"

"His name?"

"Look, I can't tell you that. He bought the car in good faith. You got no call bothering him now."

The little man said, "If I chose, I could draw the information from you in a number of ways. But never mind. I'll locate the car easily enough. And you'll certainly regret this scandalous breach of custodial duties. You certainly shall."

He went stamping out of the showroom, muttering indignantly.

Several minutes later a flash of lightning blazed across the sky. "Lightning?" the auto dealer wondered. "In January? During a snowstorm?"

When the thunder came rumbling in, every pane of plate glass in every window of the showroom shattered and fell out in the same instant.

Sam Norton sat spinning his wheels for a while in mounting fury. He knew it did no good, but he wasn't sure what else he could do, at this point, except hit the gas and hope for the car to pull itself out of the snow. His only other hope was for the highway patrol to come along, see his plight, and summon a tow truck. But the highway was all but empty, and those few cars that drove by shot past him without stopping.

When ten minutes had passed, he decided to have a closer look at the situation. He wondered vaguely if he could somehow scuff away enough snow with his foot to allow the wheels to get a little purchase. It didn't sound plausible, but there wasn't much else he could do. He got out and headed to the back of the car.

And noticed for the first time that the trunk was open.

The lid had popped up about a foot, along that neat welded line of demarcation. In astonishment Norton pushed it higher and peered inside.

The interior had a dank, musty smell. He couldn't see much of what might be in there, for the light was dim and the lid would lift no higher. It seemed to him that there were odd lumpy objects scattered about, objects of no particular size or shape, but he felt nothing when he groped around. He had the impression that the things in the trunk were moving away from his hand, vanishing into the darkest corner as he reached for them. But then his fingers encountered something cold and smooth, and he heard a welcome clink of metal on metal. He pulled.

A set of tire chains came forth.

He grinned at his good luck. Just what he needed! Quickly he unwound the chains and crouched by the back wheels of the car to fasten them in place. The lid of the trunk slammed shut as he worked—hinge must be loose, he thought—but that was of no importance. In five minutes he had the chains attached. Getting behind the wheel, he started the car again, fed some gas, delicately let out the clutch, and bit down hard on his lower lip by way of helping the car out of the snowbank. The car eased forward until it was in the clear. He left the chains on until he reached a service area eight miles up the turnpike. There he undid them; and when he stood up, he found that the trunk had popped open again. Norton tossed the chains inside and knelt in another attempt to see what else might be in the trunk, but not even squinting did he discover anything. When he touched the lid, it snapped shut, and once more the rear of the car presented that puzzling welded-tight look.

Mine is not to reason why, he told himself. He headed into the station and asked the attendant to sell him a spare tire and a set of tools. The attendant, frowning a bit, studied the car through the station window and said, "Don't know as we got one to fit. We got standards and we got smalls, but you got an in-between. Never saw a size tire like that, really."

"Maybe you ought to take a closer look," Norton suggested. "Just in case it's really a standard foreign-car size, and—"

"Nope. I can see from here. What you driving, anyway? One of them Japanese jobs?"

"Something like that."

"Look, maybe you can get a tire in Harrisburg. They got a place there, it caters to foreign cars, get yourself a muffler, shocks, anything you need."

"Thanks," Norton said, and went out.

He didn't feel like stopping when the turnoff for Harrisburg came by. It made him a little queasy to be driving without a spare, but somehow he wasn't as worried about it as he'd been before. The trunk had had tire chains when he needed them. There was no telling what else might turn up back there at the right time. He drove on.

Since the little man's own vehicle wasn't available to him, he had to arrange a rental. That was no problem, though. There were agencies in every city that specialized in such things. Very shortly he was in touch with one, not exactly by telephone, and was explaining his dilemma. "The difficulty," the little man said, "is that he's got a head start of several days. I've traced him to a point

53

west of Chicago, and he's moving forward at a pretty steady four hundred fifty miles a day."

"You'd better fly, then."

"That's what I've been thinking, too," said the little man. "What's available fast?"

"Could have given you a nice Persian job, but it's out having its tassels restrung. But you don't care much for carpets anyway, do you? I forgot."

"Don't trust 'em in the thermals," said the little man. "I caught an updraft once in Sikkim and I was halfway up the Himalayas before I got things under control. Looked for a while like I'd end up in orbit. What's at the stable?"

"Well, some pretty decent jobs. There's this classy stallion that's been resting up all winter, though actually he's a little cranky—maybe you'd prefer the bay gelding. Why don't you stop around and decide for yourself?"

"Will do," the little man said. "You still take Diner's Club, don't you?"

"All major credit cards, as always. You bet."

Norton was in southern Illinois, an hour out of St. Louis on a foggy, humid morning, when the front right-hand tire blew. He had been expecting it to go for a day and a half, now, ever since he'd stopped in Altoona for gas. The kid at the service station had tapped the tire's treads and showed him the weak spot, and Norton had nodded and asked about his chances of buying a spare, and the kid had shrugged and said, "It's a funny size. Try in Pittsburgh, maybe." He tried in Pittsburgh, killing an hour and a half there, and hearing from several men who probably ought to know that tires just weren't made to that size, nohow. Norton was beginning to wonder how the previous owner of the car had managed to find replacements. Maybe this was still the original set, he figured. But he was morbidly sure of one thing: That weak spot was going to give out, beyond any doubt, before he saw L.A.

When it blew, he was doing about 35, and he realized at once what had happened. He slowed the car to a halt without losing control. The shoulder was wide here, but even so Norton was grateful that the flat was on the right-hand side of the car; he didn't much want to feature having to change a tire with his rump to the traffic. He was still congratulating himself on that small bit of good luck when he remembered that he had no spare tire.

Somehow he couldn't get very disturbed about it. Spending a dozen hours a day behind the wheel was evidently having a tranquilizing effect on him; at this point nothing much worried him, not even the prospect of being stranded an hour east of St. Louis. He would merely walk to the nearest telephone, wherever that might happen to be, and he would phone the local automobile club and explain his predicament, and they would come out and get him and tow him to civilization. Then he would settle in a motel for a day or two, phoning Ellen at her sister's place in L.A. to say that he was all right but was going to be a little late. Either he would have the tire patched or the automobile club would find a place in St. Louis that sold odd sizes, and everything would turn out for the best. Why get into a dither?

He stepped out of the car and inspected the flat, which looked very flat indeed. Then, observing that the trunk had popped open again, he went around back. Reaching in experimentally, he expected to find the tire chains at the outer edge of the trunk, where he had left them. They weren't there. Instead his fingers closed on a massive metal bar. Norton tugged it partway out of the trunk and discovered that he had found a jack. Exactly so, he thought. And the spare tire ought to be right in back of it, over here, yes? He looked, but the lid was up only eighteen inches or so, and he couldn't see much. His fingers encountered good rubber, though. Yes, here it is. Nice and plump, brand new, deep treads—very pretty. And next to it, if my luck holds, I ought to find a chest of golden doubloons. . . .

The doubloons weren't there. Maybe next time, he told himself. He hauled out the tire and spent a sweaty half hour putting it on. When he was done, he dumped the jack, the wrench, and the blown tire into the trunk, which immediately shut to the usual hermetic degree of sealing. An hour later, without further incident, he crossed the Mississippi into St. Louis, found a room in a shiny new motel overlooking the Gateway Arch, treated himself to a hot shower and a couple of cold Gibsons, and put in a collect call to Ellen's sister. Ellen had just come back from some unsuccessful apartment hunting, and she sounded tired and discouraged. Children were howling in the background as she said, "You're driving carefully, aren't you?"

"Of course I am."

"And the new car is behaving okay?"

"Its behavior," Norton said, "is beyond reproach."

"My sister wants to know what kind it is. She says a Volvo is a good kind of car, if you want a foreign car. That's a Norwegian car."

"Swedish," he corrected.

He heard Ellen say to her sister, "He bought a Swedish car." The reply was unintelligible, but a moment later Ellen said, "She says you did a smart thing. Those Swedes, they make good cars too."

The flight ceiling was low, with visibility less than half a mile in thick fog. Airports were socked in all over Pennsylvania and eastern Ohio. The little man flew westward, though, keeping just above the fleecy whiteness spreading to the horizon. He was making good time, and it was a relief not to have to worry about those damned private planes.

The bay gelding had plenty of stamina, too. He was a fuel-guzzler, that was his only trouble. You didn't get a whole lot of miles to the bale with the horses available nowadays, the little man thought sadly. Everything was in a state of decline, and you had to accept the situation.

His original flight plan had called for him to overtake his car somewhere in the Texas panhandle. But he had stopped off in Chicago on a sudden whim to visit friends, and now he calculated he wouldn't catch up with the car until Arizona. He couldn't wait to get behind the wheel again after all these months.

The more he thought about the trunk and the tricks it had played, the more bothered by it all Sam Norton was. The chains, the spare tire, the jack—what next? In Amarillo he had offered a mechanic twenty bucks to get the trunk open. The mechanic had run his fingers along that smooth seam in disbelief. "What are you, one of those television fellers?" he asked. "Having some fun with me?"

"Not at all," Norton said. "I just want that trunk opened up."

"Well, I reckon maybe with an acetylene torch—"

But Norton felt an obscure terror at the idea of cutting into the car that way. He didn't know why the thought frightened him so much, but it did, and he drove out of Amarillo with the car whole and the mechanic muttering and spraying his boots with tobacco juice. A hundred miles on, when he was over the New Mexico border and moving through bleak, forlorn, winter-browned country, he decided to put the trunk to a test.

LAST GAS BEFORE ROSWELL, a peeling sign warned. FILL UP NOW!

The gas gauge told him that the tank was nearly empty. Roswell was somewhere far ahead. There wasn't another human being in sight, no town, not even a shack. This, Norton decided, is the right place to run out of gas.

He shot past the gas station at fifty miles an hour.

In a few minutes he was two and a half mountains away from the filling station and beginning to have doubts not merely of the wisdom of his course but even of his sanity. Deliberately letting himself run out of gas was against all reason; it was even harder to do than deliberately letting the telephone go unanswered. A dozen times he ordered himself to swing around and go back to fill his tank, and a dozen times he refused.

The needle crept lower, until it was reading *E* for empty, and still he drove ahead. The needle slipped through the red warning zone below the *E*. He had used up even the extra couple of gallons of gas that the tank didn't register—the safety margin for careless drivers. And any moment now the car would—

—stop.

For the first time in his life, Sam Norton had run out of gas. Okay, trunk, let's see what you can do, he thought. He pushed the door open and felt the chilly zip of the mountain breeze. It was quiet here, ominously so; except for the gray ribbon of the road itself, this neighborhood had a darkly prehistoric look, all sagebrush and pinyon pine and not a trace of man's impact. Norton walked around to the rear of his car.

The trunk was open again.

It figures. Now I reach inside and find that a ten-gallon can of gas has mysteriously materialized, and . . .

He couldn't feel any can of gas in the trunk. He groped a good long while and came up with nothing more useful than a coil of thick rope.

Rope?

What good is rope to a man who's out of gas in the desert?

Norton hefted the rope, seeking answers from it and not getting any. It occurred to him that perhaps this time the trunk hadn't *wanted* to help him. The skid, the blowout—those hadn't been his fault. But he had with malice aforethought let the car run out of gas, just to see what would happen, and maybe that didn't fall within the scope of the trunk's service.

Why the rope, though?

Some kind of grisly joke? Was the trunk telling him to go string himself up? He couldn't even do that properly here; there wasn't a tree in sight tall enough for a man to hang himself from, not even a telephone pole. Norton felt like kicking himself. Here he was, and here he'd remain for hours, maybe even for days, until another car came along. Of all the dumb stunts!

Angrily he hurled the rope into the air. It uncoiled as he let go of it, and one end rose straight up. The rope hovered about a yard off the ground, rigid, pointing skyward. A faint turquoise cloud formed at the upper end, and a thin, muscular olive-skinned boy in a turban and a loincloth climbed down to confront the gaping Norton.

"Well, what's the trouble?" the boy asked brusquely.

"I'm . . . out . . . of . . . gas."

"There's a filling station twenty miles back. Why didn't you tank up there?"

'I . . . that is . . ."

"What a damned fool," the boy said in disgust. "Why do I get stuck with jobs like this? All right, don't go anywhere and I'll see what I can do."

He went up the rope and vanished.

When he returned, some three minutes later, he was carrying a tin of gasoline. Glowering at Norton, he slid the gas-tank cover aside and poured in the gas.

"This'll get you to Roswell," he said. "From now on look at your dashboard once in a while. Idiot!"

He scrambled up the rope. When he disappeared, the rope went limp and fell. Norton shakily picked it up and slipped it into the trunk, whose lid shut with an aggressive slam.

Half an hour went by before Norton felt it was safe to get behind the wheel again. He paced around the car something more than a thousand times, not getting a whole lot steadier in the nerves, and ultimately, with night coming on, got in and switched on the ignition. The engine coughed and turned over. He began to drive toward Roswell at a sober and steadfast fifteen miles an hour.

He was willing to believe anything, now.

And so it did not upset him at all when a handsome reddish-brown horse with the wingspread of a DC-3 came soaring through the air, circled above the car a couple of times, and made a neat landing on the highway alongside him. The horse trotted along, keeping pace with him, while the small white-haired man in the saddle yelled, "Open your window wider, young fellow! I've got to talk to you!"

Norton opened the window.

The little man said, "Your name Sam Norton?"

"That's right."

"Well, listen, Sam Norton, you're driving my car!"

Norton saw a dirt turnoff up ahead and pulled into it. As he got out, the pegasus came trotting up and halted to let its rider dismount. It cropped moodily at sagebrush, fluttering its huge wings a couple of times before folding them neatly along its back.

The little man said, "My car, all right. Had her specially made a few years back, when I was on the road a lot. Dropped her off at the garage a year ago last November, on account of I had a business trip to make abroad, but I never figured they'd sell her out from under me before I got back. It's a decadent age, that's the truth."

"Your . . . car . . ." Norton said.

"My car, yep. Afraid I'll have to take it from you, too. Car like this, you don't want to own it, anyway. Too complicated. Get yourself a decent little standard-make flivver, eh? Well, now, let's unhitch this trailer thing of yours, and then—"

"Wait a second," Norton said. "I bought this car legally. I've got a bill of sale to prove it, and a letter from the dealer's lawyer, explaining that—"

"Don't matter one bit," said the little man. "One crook hires another crook to testify to his character, that's not too impressive. I know you're an innocent party, son, but the fact remains that the car *is* my property, and I hope I don't have to use special persuasion to get you to relinquish it."

"You just want me to get out and walk, is that it? In the middle of the New Mexico desert at sundown? Dragging the damned U-Haul with my bare hands?"

"Hadn't really considered that problem much," the little man said. "Wouldn't altogether be fair to you, would it?"

"It sure wouldn't." He thought a moment. "And what about the two hundred bucks I paid for the car?"

The little man laughed. "Shucks, it cost me more than that to rent the pegasus to come chasing you! And the overhead! You know how much hay that critter—"

"That's your problem," Norton said. "Mine is that you want to strand me in the desert and that you want to take away a car that I bought in good faith for two hundred dollars, and even if it's a goddam magic car I—"

"Hush, now," said the little man. "You're gettin' all upset, Sam! We can work this thing out. You're going to L.A., that it?"

"Ye-es."

"So am I. Okay, we travel together. I'll deliver you and your trailer there, and then the car's mine again, and you forget anything you might have seen these last few days."

"And my two hundred dol—"

"Oh, all right." The little man walked to the back of the car. The trunk opened; he slipped in a hand and pulled forth a sheaf of crisp new bills, a dozen twenties, which he handed to Norton. "Here. With a little something extra, thrown in. And don't look at them so suspiciously, hear? That's good legal tender U.S. money. They even got different serial numbers, every one." He winked and strolled over to the grazing pegasus, which he slapped briskly on the rump. "Git along, now. Head for home. You cost me enough already!"

The horse began to canter along the highway. As it broke into a gallop it spread its superb wings; they beat furiously a moment, and the horse took off, rising in a superb arc until it was no bigger than a hawk against the darkening sky, and then was gone.

The little man slipped into the driver's seat of the car and fondled the wheel with obvious affection. At a nod, Norton took the seat beside him, and off they went.

"I understand you peddle computers," the little man said when he had driven a couple of miles. "Mighty interesting things, computers. I've been considering computerizing our operation too, you know? It's a pretty big outfit, a lot of consulting stuff all over the world, mostly dowsing now, some thaumaturgy, now and then a little transmutation, things like that, and although we use traditional methods, we don't object to the scientific approach. Now, let me tell you a bit about our inventory flow, and maybe you can make a few intelligent suggestions, young fellow, and you might just be landing a nice contract for yourself . . . ."

Norton had the roughs for the system worked out before they hit Arizona. From Phoenix he phoned Ellen and found out that she had rented an apartment just outside Beverly Hills, in what *looked* like a terribly expensive neighborhood but really wasn't, at least, not by comparison with some of the other things she'd seen, and—

"It's okay," he said. "I'm in the process of closing a pretty big sale. I . . . ah . . . picked up a hitchhiker, and turns out he's thinking of going computer soon, a fairly large company—"

"Sam, you haven't been drinking, have you?"

"Not a drop."

"A hitchhiker and you sold him a computer. Next you'll tell me about the flying saucer you saw."

"Don't be silly," Norton said. "Flying saucers aren't real."

They drove into L.A. in midmorning, two days later. By then he had written the whole order, and everything was set; the commission, he figured, would be enough to see him through a new car, maybe one of those Swedish jobs Ellen's sister had heard about. The little man seemed to have no difficulty finding the address of the apartment Ellen had taken; he negotiated the maze of the freeways with complete ease and assurance, and pulled up outside the house.

"Been a most pleasant trip, young fellow," the little man said. "I'll be talking to my bankers later today about that wonderful machine of yours. Meanwhile, here we part. You'll have to unhitch the trailer, now."

"What am I supposed to tell my wife about the car I drove here in?"

"Oh, just say that you sold it to that hitchhiker at a good profit. I think she'll appreciate that."

They got out. While Norton undid the U-Haul's couplings, the little man took something from the trunk, which had opened a moment before. It was a large rubbery tarpaulin. The little man began to spread it over the car. "Give us a hand here, will you?" he said. "Spread it nice and neat, so it covers the fenders and everything." He got inside, while Norton, baffled, carefully tucked the tarpaulin into place.

"You want me to cover the windshield too?" he asked.

"Everything," said the little man, and Norton covered the windshield. Now the car was wholly hidden.

There was a hissing sound, as of air being let out of tires. The tarpaulin began to flatten. As it sank towards the ground, there came a cheery voice from underneath, calling, "Good luck, young fellow!"

In moments the tarpaulin was less than three feet high. In a minute more, it lay flat against the pavement. There was no sign of the car. It might have evaporated, or vanished into the earth. Slowly, uncomprehendingly, Norton picked up the tarpaulin, folded it until he could fit it under his arm, and walked into the house to tell his wife that he had arrived in Los Angeles.

Sam Norton never met the little man again, but he made the sale, and the commission saw him through a new car with something left over. He still has the tarpaulin, too. He keeps it folded up and carefully locked away in his basement. He's afraid to get rid of it, but he doesn't like to think of what might happen if someone came across it and spread it out.

SMELL

JOAN AIKEN

"Have you put that it's for a poor old lady who's very hard of hearing and nearly blind as well? Have you asked them to do it as quick as possible?" said Mrs. Ruffle.

She was a massive old woman; her round, soup-plate hat encircled a heavy face, fixed in the expression of stony non-communication habitual to the deaf.

"Yes, I told you so twice. I put it," her son said impatiently and then, remembering she could not hear him, gave several emphatic nods, stooping towards her over the shop's post-office counter. But she continued to watch him with an intent, peering, distrustful stare as he folded the letter he had written, tucked it among the wadding in a small sturdy cardboard box, bound up the package with adhesive tape, addressed it in large capitals to HEARING-AID REPAIR DEPARTMENT, Stanbury Ear, Nose, and Throat Hospital, Stanbury, and stuck on a stamp.

"How soon do you think they will send it back, George?"

"Three days, four maybe. *Four days*," he shouted, mouthing the words.

"What did you say, dear?"

He tried to take her hand, to demonstrate by counting on her knobby, aged fingers, but, physical contact being a rarity with her nowadays, she started back nervously, like a wild animal in hostile surroundings, and by her movement dislodged a tall pyramid of biscuit tins which stood on the floor beside her. Marie, Nice, Oval Osborne, Petit Beurre, Sponge Fingers, all came cascading down onto the uneven brick floor of the little shop. Hardly noticing the chaos she left behind her, Mrs. Ruffle tapped her way, with her heavy white-painted stick, toward the street entrance, through a group of other customers who made solicitous way for her. In the door she paused to sniff disapprovingly and say, "There's something smells not all as it should be around here. George! You've let some of the biscuits go moldy! Not putting the lid on tight, that's what does it. There's mice there, too, if you ask me. I never could fancy a Marie biscuit that's gone soft, that the mice have run over."

George Ruffle, angrily shoveling biscuits, strips of corrugated paper, and shavings off the bricks, made no answer but shrugged in response to sympathetic grins as if to say, "What can you do?" He dumped the spoiled stock in an empty wooden barrel and went back to serving customers behind the counter.

His mother put her head through the door again.

"Your father wouldn't ever have let such a thing happen! Nothing but fresh goods there was in the shop when he was living. None of this frozen stuff then, that costs double the money and doesn't do you a bit of good."

And she directed a short-sighted malignant glance at the deep freeze, installed by George after his father's death in spite of her vehemently expressed objections.

"How often d'you clean that contraption out, anyway? Every other August bank holiday? Wouldn't hurt to get that lazy boy of yours to do it once in a blue moon." She gave a grim chuckle and shook off the hand of a man who offered to help her down the two steps into the village street. "Someone around here been fishing by the smell of him," she muttered, and tapped her way out of sight.

"Independent old lady, your mother," a farmer said, buying national insurance stamps at the post-office counter.

"Independent!" said George. "You can't do a thing with her. The Health Visitor doesn't like her being out there in the cottage on her own, but she won't budge. Says she means to die among her own things, not in an old people's home that's only the workhouse by another name."

"Still, she's good for a tidy few years yet by the look of her."

"Oh, she's as healthy as they come," agreed George, rapping down a pile of coins and sliding them under the grill. "It's just that, being so deaf, she's a bit of a risk on her own—wouldn't hear a pan boil over, or a tap left running. Specially without her aid, like now. Still, what can you do? You can't shift her. She's got enough to live on, she was born in that cottage, and she reckons to die there— Yes, Wally? Postal order for three and eleven? Frank," he called to his son at the back of the shop, "just leave loading up those orders into the van and give a hand at the counter a moment, will you?"

Frank, a handsome, sullen-looking boy in white overalls, dropped the carton of groceries he had just picked up and reluctantly obeyed.

Meanwhile old Mrs. Ruffle slowly pursued her familiar course. Butcher: chopped shin and a bone for the dog. Rendell the chemist: digestive tablets. "No hearing-aid batteries today?" he inquired, but receiving absolutely no response, abandoned the attempt to communicate and handed her the tablets and change, which she carefully counted, feeling the milled edges of the sixpences with her thumbnail.

Two pairs of woollen stockings at Miss Knox's.

"She buys two pairs a month, regular," Miss Knox confided to her visiting cousin when the door closed behind Mrs. Ruffle. "Extravagant, but she says she can't see to mend, and she might as well spend her cash as let it lie."

"She must be nicely off."

"Oh, they say in the village that she's got quite a little nest-egg tucked away somewhere in that cottage of hers."

Miss Knox glanced out at the solid old back, slowly retreating along the village street.

Old Mrs. Ruffle tapped her way home by touch, sight within a four-foot radius, and smell. Whiff of scorching hair and cuticle from the blacksmith's. Steep grassy bank in front of the church. Dandelions on it. Church gate, newly painted, with a reek of warm creosote in the June sun. Stretch of yew hedge around the churchyard: a dark, dusty smell. She went through the gate into the old cemetery and checked on Bert's grave; yes, they had changed the flowers and the grass was clipped; no more than they ought to do, either, but she wouldn't ever be surprised if they left off doing it, George never having shown the proper respect for his father, Doris thinking herself a cut above her husband's family, and Frank a spoiled lazy young scamp, his mind on nothing but lotteries and motor-bikes.

After the ritual visit to the grave and ten minutes' rest on the churchyard bench (it bore a plaque in memory of Albert Edward Ruffle, donated by his widow), she went slowly on. Past the Ring of Bells: smell of sawdust and beer through the open door. Down the hill that led from the village on its knoll to the flat salt marshes below. Dark, first, between shady banks. Smell of damp earth and long grass. Then out into the sun again. Tang of ammonia borne along the breeze from the sheep pastured on the marshes beyond the dyke. When she had on her hearing aid, Mrs. Ruffle could just catch their thin, incessant bleating, but now the sound was lost to her, dispersed into the great bright vault of sky. She stumped on, sniffing the salt of the five-mile-distant sea, keeping carefully to the middle of the narrow little flat road between its neatly tended dykes. The only vehicles to pass that way were farm trucks and delivery vans; the drivers were familiar with the sight of her stocky figure ahead of them, and slowed carefully to skirt around her, two wheels on the verge.

Now she began to get the fragrance of her privet hedge, her broad beans in full flower; as she drew nearer home, the accustomed smell of the cottage itself came out to greet her: old brickwork, reed thatch, the boiled potatoes of a thousand dinners. Rover the bullterrier lumbered wagging from his kennel—so familiar was his greeting that she almost deceived herself she could hear the joyful rattle of his chain. She gave him the bone, and he settled down to worry it in a patch of dust and sun.

With unerring fingers she reached for the key, hidden on its nail under the thatch—and paused. It was hanging the wrong way around. Muttering distrustfully to herself she took it down, inserted it in the lock, and opened her front door.

The instant she stepped inside she knew that an intruder had been there—might, for all she could hear, be there still. She stood motionless, with dilated eyes and nostrils, desperately straining her blocked ears to listen, until fear and the vain concentration turned her giddy. Only after more than five minutes had gone by did she dare creep tremulously forward, turning her head from side to side like a tortoise, moving across her room from one piece of furniture to the next. Yes! That chair had been shifted, so had the table. The cupboard door was unlatched. She reached in, right to the back, and brought out a small pink lusterware teapot; with shaking fingers, she removed the lid.

The teapot was empty.

It took Mrs. Ruffle a very long time to assimilate this fact. A dozen, two dozen times she replaced the teapot, took it out again, felt inside it. Then she took out other teapots—jugs, bowls, dishes—and feverishly, uselessly hunted inside each in turn. She ransacked the whole cupboard—the room—the house. She put everything back and then started again. By the third time around she could not be bothered to replace the articles she had moved. There was no strength left in her. She sat down weakly in the bony old armchair that had adapted itself to her shape through forty years of use, and went straight to sleep. In her sleep she twitched and shivered like a dog that dreams of hunting; her hands opened and shut in a ceaseless, obsessive search.

Next morning she woke early and began searching again; then she broke off, remembering that Sid the milk boy would soon arrive, and went out to watch for him. As soon as his faded blue pony cart stopped outside she ran out to the gate.

"Sid! I've been robbed! I've been robbed, Sid! You'll have to get the police."

"Are you all right, missis?" Sid was alarmed by her haggard whiteness and vacant, unfixed look; he offered to take her along to George's in the cart, but she ignored the offer, which indeed she had not heard, and finally he drove off, promising to send help right away.

When Constable Trencher came to the cottage, she was at first reassured by his imposing dark-blue uniform and bright buttons. He searched the place, from attic bedrooms to the back cellar under the garden that was never used because the septic tank tended to flood into it in wet weather. Everywhere the constable went, Mrs. Ruffle followed.

"How are you going to get the money back?" she kept saying. "How are you going to get back my five hundred pounds? You *will* get it back, won't you?"

When he tried to explain the obstacles to this outcome: the absence of fingerprints, the lack of clues or witnesses, the fact that, although almost everybody in the village had suspected the existence of her hoard, in fact there was no proof at all that it had amounted to as much as she claimed, or even to a tenth of that figure; when he tried to lecture her on the folly of keeping five hundred pounds in a teapot, she gave no evidence of having heard him, but continued to repeat, "You will get it back, won't you?"

He wondered if she was quite right in the head, if the shock had damaged her wits. At last he appealed for guidance to his superior, Superintendent Bray, who sensibly postponed talking to her until the hospital had sent back her repaired hearing aid, and communication, if only of a patchy kind, was once more reestablished.

George, angry, embarrassed, touchy, and ashamed, escorted his mother to the police station.

"You realize it was a very foolish act, to keep all that money at home, Mrs. Ruffle?" the superintendent addressed her loudly. "We can't promise to get it back, you know."

"Don't you lecture me, young man!" the old woman snapped. "You just *do* get it back, that's all I want. He can't spend it yet a while, can he, or the neighbors will get suspicious."

"He?"

"The thief, the one who took it."

"He may have used it to pay a debt outside the district. And we haven't any clue as to who took it at present."

"Well, use your wits, you dumb-headed fool!"

"Mother!" said George, scandalized, but Mrs. Ruffle went on undeterred.

"It must be someone who comes to the house regular, mustn't it, or Rover would have kicked up a shine. Who comes to the house regular? Well, there's Sid Curtis, with the milk, young Tom Haynes the postman, my grandson Frank brings my groceries once a week, there's my son George here—"

"Mother! Really!"

"—my daughter-in-law Doris, not that *she* comes more than once in a month of Sundays, there's Wally Turner reads the electric meter, Bernard Wiggan does a bit of digging for me when the pub's shut, Alf Dunning delivers the coal, and Luke Short and Jim Hamble from the council, they come and empty out my septic tank when it chocks up. So it must be one o'them, mustn't it?"

"That's all very well, missis," the superintendent pointed out, "but that gives us quite a choice, doesn't it? Unless you have any idea which it might be?"

"Oh, I know who it is," she said scornfully. The two men gaped at her.

"What do you mean, you know, Mother? How do you know?"

"I smelled him, didn't I?"

"You *smelled* him?"

"Folks smell different, don't they? *You*," she said to the superintendent, "you smell of nice clean broadcloth. My son George mostly smells of cheese. Sid Curtis smells of pony. Tom Haynes smells of that flake tobacco he smokes; young Frank reeks of aftershave lotion, you can smell him halfway down the road; same with Wally Turner, only with him it's those pigs he keeps; Doris uses white violet scent; Bernard always smells of the chips they fry in the public bar; Alf Dunning smells o'coal and sacking, very strong; Luke and Jim they smell of sewage (poor souls, how their wives can stand it I don't know, but we've all got to live I suppose)."

"But how can you possibly be sure?"

"If I'm not sure now," said Mrs. Ruffle, "I'll be sure next time I smell him."

"So which do you think it was?"

"Huh! I'm not telling you," said Mrs. Ruffle cunningly. "Not unless you give me your promise you'll arrest him. Otherwise, what's to stop him cutting my throat first?"

"But, good heavens, we can't arrest somebody just because you say you smelled him," the superintendent exclaimed, irritable with the effort of speaking loud enough to make her hear. "A smell's not evidence."

It took him a morning's arguing to persuade her that he really did not intend to proceed on her suggestion; when George finally took her home, she had lost the temporary vigor induced by her belief that she could convince the superintendent, and relapsed into her state of semishock. She sat listlessly in her armchair, paying no attention to George, who was telling her that now she must certainly leave her cottage and move in with him and Doris. "You can't stay here alone any longer, Mother, do you understand? What'll you live on, for one thing?"

At that she roused up a little and said, "I'll live on my old-age pension, like I always have. I just won't be able to buy any new

stockings, that's all. Doris'll have to put up with mending my old
ones, whether she likes it or not. Now get along with you George,
you haven't been much use, have you? And don't you dare
mention what I told that policeman unless you want me murdered in my bed."

She locked up after the disgruntled George and then returned
to sit muttering and twitching in her armchair, staring with a set,
heavy face into the fire.

A month went by, during which time nobody in the village
gave evidence of sudden and suspicious wealth. Various people
were questioned by the police, without result; it became plain
that the matter was going to be allowed to drop. The regular
visitors paid their regular calls at Mrs. Ruffle's cottage: Sid,
Frank, Bernard came and went; Alf Dunning delivered coal,
Doris made reluctant visits to her mother-in-law with mended
stockings; the postman left an occasional card, which Mrs. Ruffle
could not read, from her married daughter in Canada. The warm
June weather turned to a cold and rainy July; water brimmed
along the dykes and lay in pools on the sodden marsh and in Mrs.
Ruffle's garden; predictably, her septic tank began to leak an
evil-smelling trickle into the cellar, and she sent a message to the
council cleansing department asking them to come and pump her
out.

And then one day at tea-time Wally Turner came to read the
electric meter.

It had been a dark, sodden afternoon; rain endlessly trickled off
the thatch and overflowed from Mrs. Ruffle's rain-water barrel;
the saturated sheep huddled together and cried dolefully out on
the marsh; Rover dozed in his kennel and Mrs. Ruffle sat by a
fistful of fire brooding about her empty teapot. Even now, she
still sometimes momentarily believed that she might have been
mistaken about her loss, and she would take the teapot from the
cupboard, lift the lid, and peer inside wistfully, as if a bundle of
notes might suddenly materialize there.

SMELL

When Wally's knock came, Mrs. Ruffle was in the back kitchen, putting on the kettle. Accustomed to opening the door and walking in if she did not answer, Wally did so on this occasion and made his way through to the narrow passage where the meter was awkwardly sited in a dark corner under the stairs, beside the cellar door.

"Good afternoon, Wally." Mrs. Ruffle's voice behind his shoulder made him start; she was wearing felt slippers, and he had not heard her come out of the kitchen.

"Hello, there, Mrs. Ruffle," he said loudly and nervously. "Not got through quite so much current then, this time, by the look."

"That's just as well, isn't it? Now all my savings are stolen, I need to cut down on spending."

"I was sorry to hear about that, Mrs. Ruffle," he shouted.

"Were you, Wally?" She came up close to him and with apparent irrelevance asked, "How are the pigs, then?" Her nostrils twitched slightly.

"Not so bad, Mrs. Ruffle, but they don't like this weather."

"Who does? I'm worried about my cellar, I can tell you; if the council don't come soon, it's going to fill right up. Have a look at it, Wally, and say if you think the water's going to fuse my electric."

"Oh, it ought to be all right," he said, "your wiring doesn't go through the cellar, does it?"

"Just the same, I wish you'd look and see, Wally."

She unlocked the cellar door and opened it, letting out a dismaying stench of wet decay. With reluctance, Wally peered down the dark steps.

"Can you see where the water's got to?"

"It's too dark," he said.

"You eyes'll get used to it in a moment. Take a step down inside."

He took a step down, she put the end of her stick against his back and gave a powerful shove. Slipping on the wet stone, he fell forward into the dark with a desperate cry, and a splash.

Mrs. Ruffle shut and relocked the door.

"That'll teach you to help yourself to other folks' savings," she shouted through the keyhole, and went back into the kitchen to finish making tea.

Wally, who had broken his leg, managed to drag himself painfully out of two feet of foul-smelling water and up the cellar stairs.

"It wasn't me, it wasn't me!" he moaned, beating on the door with his fists. And then, much later, "Anyway, you can't prove it, you bloody old hag! You'll never see your money again."

Mrs. Ruffle paid no attention. His shouts were audible only at the back of the cottage, and not very distinctly even there; in any case, she had switched off her hearing aid, and, after some consideration, dropped it from a height onto the brick floor.

Next afternoon she plodded up to the post office, through the rain.

"You'll have to send this thing back to the hospital, George," she said. "It's gone wrong again." She watched impassively while he parceled and dispatched it.

Luke Short was in the shop, and she said, "When's the council going to come and pump out my septic, Luke? The cellar's half full of water as it is; another few days of this weather, and it'll be up to the top of the steps."

"Very sorry, Mrs. Ruffle," Luke bawled at the top of his powerful lungs. "We've had such a lot of calls, I reckon we're not liable to get around to you for another four or five days at least; say next Thursday."

Uncertain whether she had understood, he took down the big post-office calendar, held it under her nose, and pointed to Thursday's date. Following his finger, she nodded slowly.

"Thursday? I'll have to be satisfied with that, then, shan't I? Thursday ought to just about do."

And she hobbled slowly off down the village.

It rained for another week. After three days Mrs. Ruffle

decided that she could unlock the cellar door. By now the stench was noticeable even when the door was shut.

So she did not bother to open it and look inside.

THE
HUNGRY HOUSE

ROBERT BLOCH

At first there were two of them—he and she, together. That's the
way it was when they bought the house.

Then *it* came. Perhaps it was there all the time, waiting for them
in the house. At any rate, it was there now. And nothing could be
done.

Moving was out of the question. They'd taken a five-year lease,
secretly congratulating themselves on the low rental. It would be
absurd to complain to the agent, impossible to explain to their
friends. For that matter, they had nowhere else to go; they had
searched for months to find a home.

Besides, at first neither he nor she cared to admit awareness of
its presence. But both of them knew it was there.

She felt it the very first evening, in the bedroom. She was sitting
in front of the high, old-fashioned mirror of her dressing table,
combing her hair. The mirror hadn't been dusted yet and it
seemed cloudy; the light above it flickered a bit, too.

So at first she thought it was just a trick of shadows or some flaw in the glass. The wavering outline behind her seemed to blur the reflection oddly, and she frowned. Then she began to experience what she often thought of as her "married feeling"—the peculiar awareness which usually denoted her husband's unseen entrance into a room she occupied.

He must be standing behind her, now. He must have come in quietly, without saying anything. Perhaps he was going to put his arms around her, surprise her, startle her. Hence the shadow on the mirror.

She turned, ready to greet him.

The room was empty. And still the odd reflection persisted, together with the sensation of a presence at her back.

She shrugged, moved her head, and made a little face at herself in the mirror. As a smile it was a failure, because the warped glass and the poor light seemed to distort her grin into something alien—into a smile that was not altogether a composition of her own face and features.

Well, it had been a fatiguing ordeal, this moving business. She flicked a brush through her hair and tried to dismiss the problem.

Nevertheless she felt a surge of relief when he suddenly entered the bedroom. For a moment she thought of telling him, then decided not to worry him over her "nerves."

He was more outspoken. It was the following morning that the incident occurred. He came rushing out of the bathroom, his face bleeding from a razor cut on the left cheek.

"Is that your idea of being funny?" he demanded, in the petulant little-boy fashion she found so engaging. "Sneaking in behind me and making faces in the mirror? Gave me an awful start—look at this nick I sliced on myself."

She sat up in bed.

"But darling, I haven't been making faces at you. I didn't stir from this bed since you got up."

"Oh." He shook his head, his frown fading into a second set of wrinkles expressing bewilderment. "Oh, I see."

"What is it?" She suddenly threw off the covers and sat on the edge of the bed, wriggling her toes and peering at him earnestly.

"Nothing," he murmured. "Nothing at all. Just thought I saw you, or somebody, looking over my shoulder in the mirror. All of a sudden, you know. It must be those damned lights. Got to get some bulbs in town today."

He patted his cheek with a towel and turned away. She took a deep breath.

"I had the same feeling last night," she confessed, then bit her lip.

"You did?"

"It's probably just the lights, as you said, darling."

"Uh-huh." He was suddenly preoccupied. "That must be it. I'll make sure and bring those new bulbs."

"You'd better. Don't forget, the gang is coming down for the housewarming on Saturday."

Saturday proved to be a long time in coming. In the interim, both of them had several experiences which served to upset their minds much more than they cared to admit.

The second morning, after he had left for work, she went out in back and looked at the garden. The place was a mess—half an acre of land, all those trees, the weeds everywhere, and the dead leaves of autumn dancing slowly around the old house. She stood off on a little knoll and contemplated the grave gray gables of another century. Suddenly she felt lonely here. It wasn't only the isolation, the feeling of being half a mile from the nearest neighbor, down a deserted dirt road. It was more as though she were an intruder here—an intruder upon the past. The cold breeze, the dying trees, the sullen sky were welcome; they belonged to the house. She was the outsider, because she was young, because she was alive.

She felt it all, but did not think it. To acknowledge her sensations would be to acknowledge fear. Fear of being alone. Or, worse still, fear of *not* being alone.

Because, as she stood there, the back door closed.

Oh, it was the autumn wind, all right. Even though the door didn't bang, or slam shut. It merely closed. But that was the wind's work, it had to be. There was nobody in the house, nobody to close the door.

She felt in her housedress pocket for the door key, then shrugged as she remembered leaving it on the kitchen sink. Well, she hadn't planned to go inside yet anyway. She wanted to look over the yard, look over the spot where the garden had been and where she fully intended a garden to bloom next spring. She had measurements to make, and estimates to take, and a hundred things to do here outside.

And yet, when the door closed, she knew she had to go in. Something was trying to shut her out, shut her out of her own house, and that would never do. Something was fighting against her, fighting against all idea of change. She had to fight back.

So she marched up to the door, rattled the knob, found herself locked out as she expected. The first round was lost. But there was always the window.

The kitchen window was eye level in height, and a small crate served to bring it within easy reach. The window was open a good four inches and she had no trouble inserting her hands to raise it further.

She tugged.

Nothing happened. The window must be stuck. But it wasn't stuck; she'd just opened it before going outside and it had opened quite easily; besides, they'd tried all the windows and found them in good operating condition.

She tugged again. This time the window raised a good six inches and then—something slipped. The window came down like the blade of a guillotine, and she got her hands out just in time. She bit her lip, sent strength through her shoulders, raised the window once more.

And this time she stared into the pane. The glass was transparent, ordinary window glass. She'd washed it just yesterday and she knew it was clean. There had been no blur, no shadow, and certainly no movement.

80

But there was movement now. Something cloudy, something obscenely opaque, peered out of the window, peered out of itself and pressed the window down against her. Something matched her strength to shut her out.

Suddenly, hysterically, she realized that she was staring at her own reflection through the shadows of the trees. Of course, it had to be her own reflection. And there was no reason for her to close her eyes and sob as she tugged the window up and half tumbled her way into the kitchen.

She was inside, and alone. Quite alone. Nothing to worry about. Nothing to worry him about. She wouldn't tell him.

He wouldn't tell her either. Friday afternoon, when she took the car and went into town for groceries and liquor in preparation for tomorrow's party, he stayed home from the office and arranged the final details of settling down.

That's why he carried up all the garment bags to the attic—to store the summer clothes, get them out of the way. And that's how he happened to open the little cubicle under the front gable. He was looking for the attic closet; he'd put down the bags and started to work along the wall with a flashlight. Then he noticed the door and the padlock.

Dust and rust told their own story; nobody had come this way for a long, long time. He thought again of Hacker, the glib real-estate agent who'd handled the rental of the place. "Been vacant several years and needs a little fixing up," Hacker had said. From the looks of it, nobody had lived here for ages. All the better; he could force the lock with a common file.

He went downstairs for the file and returned quickly, noting as he did so that the attic dust told its own story. Apparently the former occupants had left in something of a hurry—debris was scattered everywhere, and swaths and swirls scored the dust to indicate that belongings had been dragged and hauled and swept along in a haphazard fashion.

Well, he had all winter to straighten things out, and right now he'd settle for storing the garment bags. Clipping the flashlight to his belt, he bent over the lock, file in hand, and tried his skill at breaking and entering.

The lock sprung. He tugged at the door, opened it, inhaled a gust of moldy dampness, then raised the flash and directed the beam into the long, narrow closet.

A thousand silver slivers stabbed at his eyeballs. Golden, gleaming fire seared his pupils. He jerked the flashlight back, sent the beam upwards. Again, lances of light entered his eyes.

Suddenly he adjusted his vision and comprehension. He stood peering into a room full of mirrors. They hung from cords, lay in corners, stood along the walls in rows.

There was a tall, stately full-length mirror, set in a door; a pair of plate-glass ovals, inset in old-fashioned dresser-tops; a panel glass, and even a complete, dismantled bathroom medicine cabinet similar to the one they had just installed. And the floor was lined with hand-mirrors of all sizes and shapes. He noted an ornate silver-handled mirror straight from a woman's dressing table; behind it stood the vanity mirror removed from the table itself. And there were pocket mirrors, mirrors from purse compacts, mirrors of every size and shape. Against the far wall stood a whole series of looking-glass slabs that appeared to have been mounted at one time in a bedroom wall.

He gazed at half a hundred silvered surfaces, gazed at half a hundred reflections of his own bewildered face.

And he thought again of Hacker, of their inspection of the house. He had noted the absence of a medicine cabinet at the time, but Hacker had glossed over it. Somehow he hadn't realized that there were no mirrors of any sort in the house—of course, there was no furniture, but still one might expect a door panel in a place this old.

No mirrors? Why? And why were they all stacked away up here, under lock and key?

It was interesting. His wife might like some of these—that

silver-handled beauty mirror, for example. He'd have to tell her about this.

He stepped cautiously into the closet, dragging the garment bags after him. There didn't seem to be any clothes-pole here, or any hooks. He could put some up in a jiffy, though. He piled the bags in a heap, stooping, and the flashlight glittered on a thousand surfaces, sent facets of fire into his face.

Then the fire faded. The silver surfaces darkened oddly. Of course, his reflection covered them now. His reflection, and something darker. Something smoky and swirling, something that was a part of the moldy dampness, something that choked the closet with its presence. It was behind him—no, at one side—no, in front of him—all around him—it was growing and growing and blotting him out—it was making him sweat and tremble and now it was making him gasp and scuttle out of the closet and slam the door and press against it with all his waning strength, and its name was—

Claustrophobia. That was it. Just claustrophobia, a fancy name for nerves. A man gets nervous when he's cooped up in a small space. For that matter, a man gets nervous when he looks at himself too long in a mirror. Let alone *fifty* mirrors!

He stood there, shaking, and to keep his mind occupied, keep his mind off what he had just half seen, half felt, half known, he thought about mirrors for a moment. . . . About looking into mirrors. Women did it all the time. Men were different.

Men, himself included, seemed to be self-conscious about mirrors. He could remember going into a clothing store and seeing himself in one of the complicated arrangements that afforded a side and rear view. What a shock that had been, the first time—and every time, for that matter! A man looks different in a mirror. Not the way he imagines himself to be, knows himself to be. A mirror distorts. That's why men hum and sing and whistle while they shave. To keep their minds off their reflections. Otherwise they'd go crazy. What was the name of that Greek mythological character who was in love with his own image?

Narcissus, that was it. Staring into a pool for hours.

Women could do it, though. Because women never saw them-selves, actually. They saw an idealization, a vision. Powder, rouge, lipstick, mascara, eye shadow, brilliantine, or merely an emptiness to which these elements must be applied. Women were a little crazy to begin with, anyway. Had to be, to love their men.

Perhaps he'd better not tell her, after all. At least, not until he checked with the real-estate agent, Hacker. He wanted to find out about this business, anyway. Something was wrong, somewhere. Why had the previous owners stored all the mirrors up here?

He began to walk back through the attic, forcing himself to go slowly, forcing himself to think of something, anything, except the fright he'd had in the room of reflections.

Reflect on something. Reflections. Who's afraid of the big bad reflection? Another myth, wasn't it?

Vampires. They had no reflections. "Tell me the truth now, Hacker. The people who built this house—were they vampires?"

That was a pleasant thought. That was a pleasant thought to carry downstairs in the afternoon twilight, to hug to your bosom in the gloom while the floors creaked and the shutters banged and the night came down in the house of shadows where something peered around the corners and grinned at you in the mirrors on the walls.

He sat there waiting for her to come home, and he switched on all the lights, and he put the radio on too and thanked God he didn't have a television set because there was a screen and the screen made a reflection and a reflection might be something he didn't want to see.

But there was no more trouble that evening, and by the time she came home with her packages, he had himself under control. So they ate and talked quite naturally—oh, quite naturally, and if it was listening, it wouldn't know they were both afraid.

They made their preparations for the party, and called up a few people on the phone, and just on the spur of the moment he suggested inviting Hacker, too. So that was done and they went to bed. The lights were all out and that meant the mirrors were dark, and he could sleep.

Only in the morning it was difficult to shave. And he caught her, yes he caught her, putting on her makeup in the kitchen, using the little compact from her purse and carefully cupping her hands against reflections.

But he didn't tell her and she didn't tell him, and if it guessed their secrets, it kept silent.

He drove off to work and she made canapés, and if at times during the long, dark, dreary Saturday the house groaned and creaked and whispered, that was only to be expected.

The house was quiet enough by the time he came home again, and somehow, that was worse. It was as though something were waiting for night to fall. That's why she dressed early, humming all the while she powdered and primped, swirling around in front of the mirror (you couldn't see too clearly if you swirled). That's why he mixed drinks before their hasty meal and saw to it that they both had several stiff ones (you couldn't see too clearly if you drank).

And then the guests tumbled in. The Teters, complaining about the winding back road through the hills. The Valliants, exclaiming over the antique paneling and the high ceilings. The Ehrs, whooping and laughing, with Vic remarking that the place looked like something designed by Charles Addams. That was a signal for a drink, and by the time Hacker and his wife arrived, the blaring radio found ample competition from the voices of the guests.

He drank, and she drank, but they couldn't shut it out together. That remark about Charles Addams was bad, and there were other things. Little things. The Talmadges had brought flowers, and she went out to the kitchen to arrange them in a cut-glass vase. There were facets in the glass, and as she stood in the kitchen, momentarily alone, and filled the vase with water from the tap, the crystal darkened beneath her fingers, and something peered, reflected from the facets. She turned, quickly, and she was all alone. All alone, holding a hundred naked eyes in her hands.

So she dropped the vase, and the Ehrs and Talmadges and Hackers and Valliants trooped out to the kitchen, and he came too. Talmadge accused her of drinking and that was reason enough for another round. Her husband said nothing, but got another vase for the flowers. And yet he must have known, because when somebody suggested a tour of the house, he put them off.

"We haven't straightened things out upstairs yet," he said. "It's a mess, and you'd be knocking into crates and stuff."

"Who's up there now?" asked Mrs. Teter, coming into the kitchen with her husband. "We just heard an awful crash."

"Something must have fallen over," the host suggested. But he didn't look at his wife as he spoke, and she didn't look at him.

"How about another drink?" she asked. She mixed and poured hurriedly, and before the glasses were half-empty, he took over and fixed another round. Liquor helped to keep people talking, and if they talked, it would drown out other sounds.

The stratagem worked. Gradually the group trickled back into the living room in twos and threes, and the radio blared and the laughter rose and the voices babbled to blot out the noise of the night.

He poured and she served, and both of them drank, but the alcohol had no effect. They moved carefully, as though their bodies were brittle glasses—glasses without bottom—waiting to be shattered by some sudden strident sound. Glasses hold liquor, but they never get drunk.

Their guests were not glasses; they drank and feared nothing, and the drinks took hold. People moved about, and in and out, and pretty soon Mr. Valliant and Mrs. Talmadge embarked on their own private tour of the house upstairs. It was irregular and unescorted, but fortunately nobody noticed either their departure or their absence. At least, not until Mrs. Talmadge came running downstairs and locked herself in the bathroom.

Her hostess saw her pass the doorway and followed her. She rapped on the bathroom door, gained admittance, and prepared to make discreet inquiries. None were necessary. Mrs. Talmadge, weeping and wringing her hands, fell upon her.

"That was a filthy trick!" she sobbed. "Coming up and sneaking on us. The dirty louse! What I want to know is, where did he get the beard? It frightened me out of my wits."

"What's all this?" she asked—knowing all the while what it was, and dreading the words to come.

"Jeff and I were in the bedroom, just standing there in the dark, I swear it, and all at once I looked up over my shoulder at the mirror because light began streaming in from the hall. Somebody had opened the door, and I could see the glass and his face. Oh, it was my husband all right, but he had a beard on and the way he came slinking in, glaring at us—"

Sobs choked off the rest. Mrs. Talmadge trembled so that she wasn't aware of the tremors which racked the frame of her hostess. She, for her part, strained to hear the rest. "—sneaked right out again before we could do anything, but wait till I get him home—scaring the life out of me and all because he's so crazy jealous—the look on his face in the mirror—"

She soothed Mrs. Talmadge. She comforted Mrs. Talmadge. She placated Mrs. Talmadge. And all the while there was nothing to soothe or calm or placate her own agitation.

Still, both of them had restored a semblance of sanity by the time they ventured out into the hall to join the party—just in time to hear Mr. Talmadge's agitated voice booming out over the excited responses of the rest.

"So I'm standing there in the bathroom and this old witch comes up and starts making faces over my shoulder in the mirror. What gives here, anyway? What kind of a house are you running here?"

Talmadge thought it was funny. So did the others. Most of the others. The host and hostess stood there, not daring to look at each other. Their smiles were cracking. Glass is brittle.

"I don't believe you!" Gwen Hacker's voice. She'd had one, or perhaps three, too many. "I'm going up right now and see for myself." She winked at her host and moved towards the stairs.

"Hey, hold on!" He was too late. She swept, or wobbled, past him.

"Halloween pranks," said Talmadge, nudging him. "Old babe in a fancy hairdo. Saw her plain as day. What you cook up for us here, anyhow?"

He began to stammer something, anything, to halt the flood of foolish babbling. She moved close to him, wanting to listen, wanting to believe, wanting to do anything but think of Gwen Hacker upstairs, all alone upstairs looking into a mirror and waiting to see—

The screams came then. Not sobs, not laughter, but screams. He took the stairs two at a time. Fat Mr. Hacker was right behind him, and the others straggled along, suddenly silent. There was the sound of feet clubbing the staircase, the sound of heavy breathing, and over everything the continuing high-pitched shriek of a woman confronted with terror too great to contain.

It oozed out of Gwen Hacker's voice, oozed out of her body as she staggered and half fell into her husband's arms in the hall. The light was streaming out of the bathroom, and it fell upon the mirror that was empty of all reflection, fell upon her face that was empty of all expression.

They crowded around the Hackers—he and she were on either side and the others clustered in front—and they moved along the hall to her bedroom and helped Mr. Hacker stretch his wife out on the bed. She had passed out, somebody mumbled something about a doctor, and somebody else said, "No, never mind, she'll be all right in a minute," and somebody else said, "Well, I think we'd better be getting along."

For the first time everybody seemed to be aware of the old house and the darkness, and the way the floors creaked and the windows rattled and the shutters banged.

Everyone was suddenly sober, solicitous, and extremely anxious to leave.

Hacker bent over his wife, chafing her wrists, forcing her to swallow water, watching her whimper her way out of emptiness. The host and hostess silently procured hats and coats and listened to expressions of polite regret, hasty farewells, and poorly formulated pretenses of "had a marvelous time, darling."

Teters, Valliants, Talmadges were swallowed up in the night. He and she went back upstairs, back to the bedroom and the Hackers. It was too dark in the hall, and too light in the bedroom. But there they were, waiting. And they didn't wait long.

Mrs. Hacker sat up suddenly and began to talk. To her husband, to them.

"I saw her," she said. "Don't tell me I'm crazy, I saw her! Standing on tiptoe behind me, looking right into the mirror. With the same blue ribbon in her hair, the one she wore the day she—"

"Please, dear," said Mr. Hacker.

She didn't please. "But I *saw* her. Mary Lou! She made a face at me in the mirror, and she's dead, you know she's dead, she disappeared three years ago and they never did find the body—"

"Mary Lou Dempster." Hacker was a fat man. He had two chins. Both of them wobbled.

"She played around here, you know she did, and Wilma Dempster told her to stay away, she knew all about this house, but she wouldn't, and now—oh, her face!"

More sobs. Hacker patted her on the shoulder. He looked as though he could stand a little shoulder-patting himself. But nobody obliged. He stood there, she stood there, still waiting. Waiting for the rest.

"Tell them," said Mrs. Hacker. "Tell them the truth."

"All right, but I'd rather get you home."

"I'll wait. I want you to tell them. You must, now."

Hacker sat down heavily. His wife leaned against his shoulder. The two waited another moment. Then it came.

"I don't know how to begin, how to explain," said fat Mr.

89

Hacker. "It's probably my fault, of course, but I didn't know. All this foolishness about haunted houses—nobody believes that stuff anymore, and all it does is push property values down, so I didn't say anything. Can you blame me?"

"I saw her face," whispered Mrs. Hacker.

"I know. And I should have told you. About the house, I mean. Why it hasn't been rented for twenty years. Old story in the neighborhood, and you'd have heard it sooner or later anyway, I guess."

"Get on with it," said Mrs. Hacker. She was suddenly strong again and he, with his wobbling chins, was weak.

Host and hostess stood before them, brittle as glass, as the words poured out; poured out and filled them to overflowing. He and she, watching and listening, filling up with the realization, with the knowledge, with that for which they had waited.

It was the Bellman house they were living in, the house Job Bellman built for his bride back in the sixties; the house where his bride had given birth to Laura and taken death in exchange. And Job Bellman had toiled through the seventies as his daughter grew to girlhood, rested in complacent retirement during the eighties as Laura Bellman blossomed into the reigning beauty of the county—some said the state, but then flattery came quickly to men's lips in those days.

There were men aplenty, coming and going through that decade; passing through the hall in polished boots, bowing and stroking brilliantined mustachios, smirking at old Job, grinning at the servants, and gazing in moonstruck adoration at Laura.

Laura took it all as her rightful due, but land's sakes, she'd never think of it, no not while Papa was still alive, and no, she couldn't, she was much too young to marry, and why, she'd never heard of such a thing, she'd always thought it was so much nicer just being friends—

Moonlight, dances, parties, hayrides, sleighrides, candy, flowers, gifts, tokens, cotillion balls, punch, fans, beauty spots, dressmakers, curlers, mandolins, cycling, and the years that whirled away. And then, one day, old Job lay dead in the four-poster bed upstairs, and the doctor came and the minister, and then the lawyer, hack-hack-hacking away with his dry, precise little cough, and his talk of inheritance and estate and annual income.

Then she was all alone, just she and the servants and the mirrors. Laura and her mirrors. Mirrors in the morning, and the careful inspection, the scrutiny that began the day. Mirrors at night before the caller arrived, before the carriage came, before she whirled away to another triumphal entry, another fan-fluttering, pirouetting descent of the staircase. Mirrors at dawn, absorbing the smiles, listening to the secrets, the tale of the evening's triumph.

"Mirror, mirror on the wall, who is the fairest of them all?"

Mirrors told her the truth, mirrors did not lie, mirrors did not paw or clutch or whisper or demand in return for acknowledgement of beauty.

Years passed, but the mirrors did not age, did not change. And Laura did not age. The callers were fewer and some of them were oddly altered. They seemed older, somehow. And yet how could that be? For Laura Bellman was still young. The mirrors said so, and they always told the truth. Laura spent more and more time with the mirrors. Powdering, searching for wrinkles, tinting and curling her long hair. Smiling, fluttering eyelashes, making deliciously delicate little moues. Swirling daintily, posturing before her own perfection.

Sometimes, when the callers came, she sent word that she was not at home. It seemed silly, somehow, to leave the mirrors. And after a while, there weren't many callers to worry about. Servants came and went, some of them died, but there were always new ones. Laura and the mirrors remained. The nineties were truly gay, but in a way other people wouldn't understand. How Laura laughed, rocking back and forth on the bed, sharing her giddy secrets with the glass!

The years fairly flew by, but Laura merely laughed. She giggled and tittered when the servants spoke to her, and it was easier now to take her meals on a tray in her room. Because there was something wrong with the servants, and with Dr. Turner who came to visit her and who was always being tiresome about her going away for a rest to a lovely home.

They thought she was getting old, but she wasn't—the mirrors didn't lie. She wore the false teeth and the wig to please the others, the outsiders, but she didn't really need them. The mirrors told her she was unchanged. They talked to her now, the mirrors did, and she never said a word. Just sat nodding and swaying before them in the room reeking of powder and patchouli, stroking her throat and listening to the mirrors telling her how beautiful she was and what a belle she would be if she would only waste her beauty on the world. But she'd never leave here, never; she and the mirrors would always be together.

And then came the day they tried to take her away, and they actually laid hands upon her—upon her, Laura Bellman, the most exquisitely beautiful woman in the world! Was it any wonder that she fought, clawed and kicked and whined, and struck out so that one of the servants crashed headlong into the beautiful glass and struck his foolish head and died, his nasty blood staining the image of her perfection?

Of course it was all a stupid mistake and it wasn't her fault, and Dr. Turner told the magistrate so when he came to call. Laura didn't have to see him, and she didn't have to leave the house. But they always locked the door to her room now, and they took away all her mirrors.

They *took away* all her mirrors!

They left her alone, caged up, a scrawny, wizened, wrinkled old woman with no reflection. They took the mirrors away and made her old; old, and ugly, and afraid.

The night they did it, she cried. She cried and hobbled around the room, stumbling blindly in a tearsome tour of nothingness.

That's when she realized she was old, and nothing could save her. Because she came up against the window and leaned her wrinkled forehead against the cold, cold glass. The light came from behind her, and as she drew away, she could see her reflection in the window.

The window—it was a mirror, too! She gazed into it, gazed long and lovingly at the tear-streaked face of the fantastically rouged and painted old harridan, gazed at the corpse-countenance readied for the grave by a mad embalmer.

Everything whirled. It was her house, she knew every inch of it, from the day of her birth onwards, the house was a part of her. It was her room, she had lived here for ever and ever. But *this*—this obscenity—was not her face. Only a mirror could show her that, and there would never be a mirror for her again. For an instant she gazed at the truth and then, mercifully, the gleaming glass of the windowpane altered and once again she gazed at Laura Bellman, the proudest beauty of them all. She drew herself erect, stepped back, and whirled into a dance. She danced forward, a prim self-conscious smile on her lips. Danced into the windowpane, half through it, until razored splinters of glass tore her scrawny throat.

That's how she died and that's how they found her. The doctor came, and the servants and the lawyer did what must be done. The house was sold, then sold again. It fell into the hands of a rental agency. There were tenants, but not for long. They had troubles with mirrors.

A man died—of a heart attack, they said—while adjusting his necktie before the bureau one evening. Grotesque enough, but he had complained to people in the town about strange happenings, and his wife babbled to everyone.

A schoolteacher who rented the place in the thirties "passed away" in circumstances which Doctor Turner had never seen fit to relate. He had gone to the rental agency and begged them to take the place off the market; that was almost unnecessary, for the Bellman home had its reputation firmly established by now.

Whether or not Mary Lou Dempster had disappeared here would never be known. But the little girl had last been seen a year ago on the road leading to the house and although a search had been made and nothing discovered, there was talk aplenty.

Then the new heirs had stepped in, briskly, with their pooh-poohs and their harsh dismissals of advice, and the house had been cleaned and put up for rental.

So he and she had come to live there—with it. And that was the story, all of the story.

Mr. Hacker put his arm around Gwen, harrumphed, and helped her rise. He was apologetic, he was shame-faced, he was deferential. Hacker's eyes never met those of his tenant.

He barred the doorway. "We're getting out of here, right now," he said. "Lease or no lease."

"That can be arranged. But—I can't find you another place tonight, and tomorrow's Sunday—"

"We'll pack and get out of here tomorrow," she spoke up. "Go to a hotel, anywhere. But we're leaving."

"I'll call you tomorrow," said Hacker. "I'm sure everything will be all right. After all, you've stayed here through the week and nothing, I mean nobody has—"

His words trailed off. There was no point in saying any more. The Hackers left and they were all alone. Just the two of them.

Just the *three* of them, that is.

But now they—he and she—were too tired to care. The inevitable letdown, product of overindulgence and overexcitement, was at hand.

They said nothing, for there was nothing to say. They heard nothing, for the house—and it—maintained a somber silence.

She went to her room and undressed. He began to walk around the house. First he went to the kitchen and opened a drawer next to the sink. He took a hammer and smashed the kitchen mirror.

Tinkle-tinkle. And then a crash! That was the mirror in the hall.

Then upstairs, to the bathroom. Crash and clink of broken glass in the medicine cabinet. Then a smash as he shattered the panel in his room. And now he came to her bedroom and swung the hammer against the huge oval of the vanity, shattering it to bits.

He wasn't cut, wasn't excited, wasn't upset. And the mirrors were gone. Every last one of them was gone.

They looked at each other for a moment. Then he switched off the lights, tumbled into bed beside her, and sought sleep.

The night wore on.

It was all a little silly in the daylight. But she looked at him again in the morning, and he went into his room and hauled out the suitcases. By the time she had breakfast ready, he was already laying his clothes out on the bed. She got up after eating and took her own clothes from the drawers and hangers and racks and hooks. Soon he'd go up to the attic and get the garment bags. The movers could be called tomorrow, or as soon as they had a destination in mind.

The house was quiet. If it knew their plans, it wasn't acting. The day was gloomy and they kept the lights off without speaking—although both of them knew it was because of the windowpanes and the story of the reflection. He could have smashed the window glass of course, but it was all a little silly. And they'd be out of here shortly.

Then they heard the noise. Trickling, burbling. A splashing sound. It came from beneath their feet. She gasped.

"Water-pipe—in the basement," he said, smiling and taking her by the shoulders.

"Better take a look." She moved towards the stairs.

"Why should you go down there? I'll tend to it."

But she shook her head and pulled away. It was her penance for gasping. She had to show she wasn't afraid. She had to show him—and it, too.

"Wait a minute," he cried. "I'll get the pipe-wrench. It's in the trunk in the car." He went out the back door. She stood irresolute, then headed for the cellar stairs. The splashing was getting louder. The burst pipe was flooding the basement. It made a funny noise, like laughter.

He could hear it even when he walked up the driveway and opened the trunk of the car. These old houses always had something wrong with them; he might have known it. Burst pipes and—

Yes. He found the wrench. He walked back to the door, listening to the water gurgle, listening to his wife scream.

She *was* screaming! Screaming down in the basement, screaming down in the dark.

He ran, swinging the heavy wrench. He clumped down the stairs, down into the darkness, the screams tearing up at him. She was caught, it had her, she was struggling with it but it was too strong, too strong, and the light came streaming in on the pool of water beside the shattered pipe and in the reflection he saw her face and the blackness of other faces swirling around her and holding her.

He brought the wrench up, brought it down on the black blur, hammering and hammering and hammering until the screaming died away. And then he stopped and looked down at her. The dark blur had faded away into the reflection of the water—the reflection that had evoked it. But she was still there, and she was still, and she would be still forever now. Only the water was getting red, where her head rested in it. And the end of the wrench was red, too.

For a moment he started to tell her about it, and then he realized she was gone. Now there were only the two of them left. He and it.

And he was going upstairs. He was walking upstairs, still carrying the bloody wrench, and he was going over to the phone to call the police and explain.

He sat down in a chair before the phone, thinking about what he'd tell them, how he'd explain. It wouldn't be easy. There was this madwoman, see, and she looked into mirrors until there was more of her alive in her reflection than there was in her own body. So when she committed suicide she lived on, somehow, and came alive in mirrors or glass or anything that reflected. And she killed others or drove them to death and their reflections were somehow joined with hers so that this thing kept getting stronger and stronger, sucking away at life with that awful core of pride that could live beyond death. Woman, thy name is vanity! And that, gentlemen, is why I killed my wife.

Yes, it was a fine explanation, but it wouldn't hold water. *Water*—the pool in the basement had evoked it. He might have known it if only he'd stopped to think, to reflect. *Reflect*. That was the wrong word, now. Reflect. The way the windowpane before him was reflecting.

He stared into the glass now, saw it behind him, surging up from the shadows. He saw the bearded man's face, the peering, pathetic, empty eyes of a little girl, the goggling grimacing stare of an old woman. It wasn't there, behind him, but it was alive in the reflection, and as he rose he gripped the wrench tightly. It wasn't there, but he'd strike at it, fight at it, come to grips with it somehow.

He turned, moving back, the ring of shadow-faces pressing. He swung the wrench. Then he saw *her* face coming up through all the rest. Her face, with shining splinters where the eyes should be. He couldn't smash it down, he couldn't hit her again.

It moved forward. He moved back. His arm went out to one side. He heard the tinkle of window glass behind him and vaguely remembered that this was how the old woman had died. The way he was dying now—falling through the window and cutting his throat—and the pain lanced up and in, tearing at his brain as he hung there on the jagged spikes of glass, bleeding his life away.

Then he was gone.

His body hung there, but he was gone.

There was a little puddle on the floor, moving and growing. The light from outside shone on it, and there was a reflection.

Something emerged fully from the shadows now, emerged and

capered demurely in the darkness.

It had the face of an old woman and the face of a child, the face of a bearded man, and *his* face, and *her* face, changing and blending.

It capered and postured, and then it squatted, dabbling. Finally, all alone in the empty house, it just sat there and waited. There was nothing to do now but wait for the next to come. And meanwhile, it could always admire itself in that growing, growing red reflection on the floor. . . .

DID YOU SEE
THE WINDOW-CLEANER?

JOHN EDGELL

Craddock was glad to be working in new offices. There was more floor space, and plenty of room to lay out the filing cabinets and the typists' desks. People always worked better when they had more space, and Craddock himself was very pleased with his own room—the first time he had had one for himself. He liked to walk in and out of the door that had his name on the window in gold lettering, and liked to receive visitors opposite his new desk.

He specially liked his swivel armchair. Not only was it a proud symbol of his executive status, it enabled him to swing around and look out the large picture window behind his desk. When he had a lot to think about, he would swivel around and fix his eyes on the traffic and pedestrians, scurrying like ants in the High Street, eight storeys below.

In the new office, there was much to organize. As the assistant office manager, it was Craddock's task to work out the new office routines, and to supervise the flow of work among the secretaries and typists. Although Forster was, strictly speaking, the boss,

Craddock knew that the efficient running of the office depended on his methods.

One of the things that Craddock specially liked about the new office was the central heating and the double-glazed windows. In the old place, as he now called it, the winters had been penetratingly cold. The icy winds had found their way through nooks and crannies, and through the window frames, bringing the temperature down to a level which not even the two-bar electric fire had been able to raise. And in the summer, the tiny cramped office had become unbearably hot, which was even more unpleasant because of the office rule that the men had to keep their jackets on.

Now all that was changed. Although this March had brought its usual share of wind, rain and fog, the new offices were as pleasant to work in as if it had been a bright spring day.

Craddock explained all this to the first visitor in his new office, a man called Cunningham who wanted the contract to clean the windows. After a few minutes of polite conversation, Craddock said:

"I would like you to meet Mr. Forster, our office manager. I think he will be able to help you better than I can on this particular matter."

When Mr. Cunningham had gone, Craddock returned to his office to study some papers and dictate his afternoon's correspondence. As he opened his door, he was surprised to see a window-cleaner already at work on his picture window. The window-cleaner was seated on a wooden cradle, suspended by ropes and pulleys immediately outside the building. He had with him a chamois cloth, and two small buckets of water. He was wearing a very outmoded jacket.

Craddock, who believed in good office relations, waved at him cheerfully as he went to his desk. But the window-cleaner took no notice, and went on polishing the sides and corners of the window.

Craddock sat down with his back to the window, and began to

study the papers. After a few minutes he had finished, and switched on his dictating machine and began dictating some letters. One of the letters was causing him difficulty. It was a case where he had to show a mixture of tact and firmness, and he was not sure how he should phrase it. He leaned back in his chair, and looked up.

He was surprised to see Mr. Cunningham staring through his glass door, as if he had been standing there several minutes. The gold lettering was outlined against his coat. A moment later, Mr. Cunningham straightened himself and moved away from the glass door, out of sight.

Craddock returned to his dictating machine. He had the strangest feeling that the window-cleaner had been staring at him, too.

The following afternoon, the buzzer rang on Craddock's desk. It was Mr. Forster.

"Would you mind coming in for a moment please, Craddock?"

"Yes, right away," he said.

He swivelled himself from his desk and walked on the fitted carpeting around to Mr. Forster's office. He knocked on the door. Mr. Forster's door was plain wood; it did not have a glass panel in it.

"Oh, Craddock, I wanted to have a word with you. It's about the window-cleaning for the office. Mr. Cunningham who came in yesterday operates a window-cleaning service, and left me with some estimates of the cost of having our windows cleaned twice a month. Here are the estimates."

Mr. Forster passed some pink papers over the desk. He said: "Can you arrange for the estimates to be accepted, and issue the instructions to the accounts department?"

Craddock took the papers and looked at them. At the top one of them read: The Cunningham Window-cleaning Company Limited. Free estimates gladly given.

Craddock thought of his smart new office with the desk and the swivel chair. He thought of the double-glazed windows, and he thought of the window-cleaner.

"They've already started work on my windows, Mr. Forster."

"We haven't got any window-cleaners yet."

"But yesterday afternoon, I had the windows in my office cleaned. There was a window-cleaner working from a cradle outside the building."

"You must be mistaken, Craddock. There are no window-cleaners yet."

Craddock silently put the papers in order.

"Make sure you inform the accounts department," said Forster as Craddock was leaving the room. He added: "My windows are filthy, so let's have them start as soon as possible."

It was a Monday morning, and Craddock was late for work. He hurried out of the bus, and walked rapidly along the High Street. The offices were at the other end of the street, and over the last month he had timed the walk as being one of six minutes.

Everyone else seemed to be late, too. The traffic rushed past with no thought for the pedestrians, many of whom recklessly jumped off the pavement and jay-walked across the street. At a zebra crossing, a policeman in a white coat and helmet was trying hard to keep his temper. A passer-by bumped into Craddock just as he was about to step onto the zebra crossing, nearly knocking him into the path of an oncoming van. The van hooted, and the car behind the van hooted as well. Craddock was the last of the pedestrians to cross the zebra, and felt the wind of the traffic behind him as he found the safety of the pavement.

The office building was directly opposite, and high up beyond the noise, Craddock could make out his own window, which overlooked the High Street. The windows glinted in the bright morning sun. I would not like to be a window-cleaner, he thought. There were no cradles on the wall of the building.

He took the elevator up to the eighth floor, and crossed the reception office towards his own office door. He had a strange premonition that the same window-cleaner would be there. He walked to his office, and there behind the picture window he saw him. As before, he was swinging in a wooden cradle.

Craddock walked over to his desk and waved, but as before the window-cleaner ignored him. Craddock cautiously sat down with his back turned to the window. The window-cleaner must be one of Cunningham's staff, mustn't he? Or must he? How had he begun work so quickly? Craddock began to feel a sense of apprehension. He knew it was the same man that he had seen before. Trying to appear uninterested, he swivelled slowly around so that he could look again. Yes: It was the same man—he had the same rather pale and sad expression, the same blank and hopeless eyes. Well, he thought, this is none of my business. He swivelled around again, and began to open his morning mail. There must be a logical explanation, he thought, I do not believe in ghosts.

Just then, he happened to glance up, and saw the figure of Cunningham staring again through his glass door. Perhaps he had come to see Mr. Forster again about the window-cleaning. It really was very odd. Craddock began to wonder whether he should mention it to Mr. Forster. How could the window-cleaner outside his own window be employed by Mr. Cunningham? Craddock was sure he had seen him when Cunningham had first visited the office. Could it have been a free trial window-cleaning offer? It did not sound likely; Mr. Forster had mentioned nothing about it. In fact, he had said in that unpleasant clear voice of his, "We haven't got any window-cleaners." Something, Craddock thought, was wrong.

A terrible scream shattered his thought. He swivelled around in his chair and was just in time to see the window-cleaner flailing his arms, staggering on the edge of the wooden cradle. His face was white and terror-stricken, and the cradle toppled over like a coracle in a storm, and the window-cleaner plunged out of sight.

Craddock jumped to his feet and rushed out of his office into

103

the elevator, just as the door was closing. Cunningham was nowhere to be seen. When the elevator reached the ground floor, Craddock elbowed his way through the other passengers and raced to the main door of the building and out into the street. A woman walked by, pushing a pram.

He dashed to the street front of the office block, and looked rapidly in every direction. A few pedestrians walked slowly by, looking in shop windows, holding their shopping baskets. Nothing! Craddock's heart beat furiously. Nothing!

He saw a policeman approaching. He ran up, sweating heavily, and gasped: "There's been a terrible accident!" And clutching the pain in his side, "The window-cleaner! He fell from up there—outside my window!"

The policeman looked where Craddock pointed. A look of cautious sympathy came into his eye.

"A window-cleaner," he said.

"Yes," panted Craddock. "Didn't you see the window-cleaner?"

"I saw no window-cleaner," said the policeman carefully. "Why don't you come with me to the station, and you can make a full report and have a cup of tea. The only window-cleaner accident around here happened years ago."

Craddock looked helplessly about. The window-cleaner had gone—he was nowhere to be seen—he couldn't be rescued. A tear fell down his cheek.

"All right, officer, I'll come with you."

In the police station, the desk sergeant took a full report of what Craddock had seen. He noted Craddock's place of work and his home address, and asked where his parents lived. Then he let Craddock go.

When Craddock wearily returned to his office, he found Mr. Forster pacing irritably up and down the room.

"Oh, Craddock, where the devil have you been? I wanted to speak to you."

"Yes, sir."

"Look, it's about this window-cleaning. Mr. Cunningham seems to have let us down. The window-cleaner he promised never turned up, and we have been unable to trace the whereabouts of his company. The telephone number on their notepaper seems to have been out of use for years."

"But didn't Mr. Cunningham come to see you today?" said Craddock.

"See me? Why, no. Should he have done?"

Mr. Forster looked up at Craddock. "Why, what on earth's the matter with you, boy?"

With a great effort, Craddock straightened himself, and said, "Nothing, sir."

"All right, then. Now, since we have been let down in this matter, we shall have to find a new window-cleaner."

"A *new* window-cleaner?" said Craddock, with careful emphasis.

Mr. Forster stared thoughtfully for several moments out of Craddock's gleaming picture window. A cloth lay on the ledge outside.

"Well, anyway," he said at length, "a window-cleaner."

THE SKYLIGHT

⚜

PENELOPE MORTIMER

The heat, as the taxi spiralled the narrow hill bends, became more violent. The road thundered between patches of shade thrown by overhanging rock. Behind the considerable noise of the car, the petulant hooting at each corner, the steady *tick-tick* of the cicadas spread through the woods and olive groves as though to announce their coming.

The woman sat so still in the back of the taxi that at corners her whole body swayed, rigid as a bottle in a jolting bucket, and sometimes fell against the five-year-old boy who curled, thumb plugged in his mouth, on the seat beside her. The woman felt herself disintegrate from heat. Her hair, tallow blonde, crept on her wet scalp. Her face ran off the bone like water off a rock—the bridges of nose, jaw and cheekbones must be drained of flesh by now. Her body poured away inside the too-tight cotton suit and only her bloodshot feet, almost purple in the torturing sandals, had any kind of substance.

"When are we there?" the boy asked.

107

"Soon."

"In a minute will we be there?"

"Yes."

A long pause. What shall we find? the mother asked herself. She wished, almost at the point of tears, that there were someone else to ask, then answer, this question.

"Are we at France now?"

For the sixth time since the plane had landed, she answered, "Yes, Johnny."

The child's eyes, heavy-lidded, long-lashed, closed; the thumb stoppered his drooping mouth. Oh, no, she thought, don't let him, he mustn't go to sleep.

"Look. Look at the . . ." Invention failed her. They passed a shack in a stony clearing. "Look at the chickens," she said, pulling at the clammy stuff of her jacket. "French chickens," she added, long after they had gone by. She stared dully at the taxi-driver's back, the dark stain of sweat between his shoulder-blades. He was not the French taxi-driver she had expected. He was old and quiet and burly, driving his cab with care. The price he had quoted for this forty-kilometer drive from the airport had horrified her. She had to translate all distances into miles and then apply them, a lumbering calculation, to England. How much, she had wanted to ask, would an English taxi-driver charge to take us from London Airport to . . .? It was absurd. There was no one to tell her anything. Only the child asking his interminable questions, with faith.

"Where?" he demanded suddenly, sitting up.

She felt herself becoming desperate. It's too much for me, she thought. I can't face it. "What do you mean—where?"

"The chickens."

"Oh. They've gone. Perhaps there'll be some more, later on."

"But when are we there?"

"Oh *Jonathan* . . ." In her exasperation, she used his full name. He turned his head away, devouring his thumb. When her hot, stiff body fell against him, he did not move. She tried to compose herself, to resume command.

It had seemed so sensible, so economical, to take this house for the summer. We all know, she had said (although she herself did not), what the French are—cheat you at every turn. And then, the horror of those Riviera beaches. We've found this charming little farmhouse up in the mountains—well, they say you can nip down to Golfe Juan in ten minutes. In the car, of course. Philip will be driving the girls, but I shall take Johnny by air. I couldn't face those dreadful hotels with him. Expensive? But, my dear, you don't *know* what it cost us in Bournemouth last year, and I feel one owes them the sun. And then there's this dear old couple, the Gachets, thrown in so to speak. They'll have it all ready for us, otherwise of course I couldn't face arriving there alone with Johnny. As it is, we shall be nicely settled when Philip and the girls arrive. I envy us too. I couldn't face the prospect of those awful public meals with Johnny—no, I just couldn't face it.

And so on. It was a story she had made up in the cold, well-ordered English spring. She could hear herself telling it. Now it was real. She was inadequate. She was in pain from the heat, and not a little afraid. The child depended on her. I can't face it, she thought, anticipating the arrival at the strange house, the couple, the necessity of speaking French, the task of getting the child bathed and fed and asleep. Will there be hot water, mosquitoes, do they know how to boil an egg? Her head beat with worry. She looked wildly from side to side of the taxi, searching for some sign of life. The woods had ended, and there was now no relief from the sun. An ugly pink house with green shutters stood away from the road; it looked solid, like an enormous brick, in its plot of small vines. Can that be it? But the taxi drove on.

"I suppose he knows where he's going," she said.

The child turned on his back, as though in bed, straddling his thin legs. Over the bunched hand his eyes regarded her darkly, unblinking.

"Do sit *up*," she said. His eyelids drooped again. His legs, his feet in their white socks and disproportionately large brown sandals, hung limp. His head fell to one side. "Poor baby," she said softly. "Tired baby." She managed to put an arm around him. They sat close, in extreme discomfort.

Suddenly, without warning, the driver swung the taxi off the road. The woman fell on top of the child, who struggled for a moment before managing to free himself. He sat up, alert, while his mother pulled and pushed, trying to regain her balance. A narrow, stony track climbed up into a bunch of olive trees. The driver played his horn around each bend. Then, on a perilous slope, the car stopped. The driver turned in his seat, searching back over his great soaked shoulder as though prepared, even expecting, to find his passengers gone.

"La Caporale," he said.

The woman bent, peering out of the car windows. She could see nothing but stones and grass. The heat seized the stationary taxi, turning it into a furnace.

"But—where?"

He indicated something which she could not see, then hauled himself out of the driving seat, lumbered around and opened the door.

"*Ici?*" she asked, absolutely disbelieving.

He nodded, spoke, again waved an arm, pointing.

"*Mais* . . ." It was no good. "He says we're here," she told the child. "We'd better get out."

They stood on the stony ground, looking about them. There was a black barn, its doors closed. There was a wall of loose rocks piled together. The cicadas screeched. There was nothing.

"But where's the house?" she demanded. "Where is the house? *Où est la maison?*"

The driver picked up their suitcases and walked away. She took the child's hand, pulling him after her. The high heels of her sandals twisted on the hard rubble; she hurried, bent from the waist, as though on bound feet. Then, suddenly remembering, she stopped and pulled out of her large new handbag a linen hat.

She fitted this, hardly glancing at him, on the child's head. "Come on," she said. "I can't think where he's taking us."

Round the end of the wall, over dead grass; and above them, standing on a terrace, was the square grey house, its shuttered windows set anyhow into its walls like holes in a warren. A small skylight, catching the sun, flashed from the mean slate roof.

They followed the driver up the steps on to the terrace. A few pots and urns stood about, suggesting that somebody had once tried to make a garden. A withered hosepipe lay on the ground as though it had died trying to reach the sparse geraniums. A chipped, white-painted table and a couple of wrought-iron chairs were stacked under a palm tree. A lizard skittered down the front of the house. The shutters and the door were of heavy black timber with iron bars and hinges. They were all closed. The heat sang with the resonant hum of failing consciousness. The driver put the suitcases down outside the closed door and wiped his face and the back of his neck with a handkerchief.

"*Vous avez la clef, madame?*"

"*La clay? La clay?*"

He pursed and twisted his hand over the lock.

"Oh, the key. No. *Non.* Monsieur and Madame Gachet . . . the people who live in the house . . . *Ce n'est pas*," she tried desperately, "*ferme.*"

The driver tried the door. It was firm. She knocked. There was no answer.

"*Vous n'avez la clef?*" He was beginning to sound petulant.

"*Non. Non. Parce que* . . . Oh *dear.*" She looked up at the blind face of the house. "They must be out. Perhaps they didn't get my wire. Perhaps . . ." She looked at the man, who did not understand what she was saying; at the child, who was simply waiting for her to do something. "I don't know *what* to do. Monsieur and Madame Gachet . . ." She pushed back her damp hair. "But I wrote to them weeks ago. My husband wrote to them. They *can't* be out."

She lifted the heavy knocker and again hammered it against the door. They waited, at first alertly, then slackening, the woman losing hope, the driver and the child losing interest. The driver spoke. She understood that he was going and wished to be paid.

"But you can't leave us like this. Supposing they don't get back for hours? Can't you help us to get in?"

He looked at her stolidly. Furious with him, humiliated by his lack of chivalry, she ran to one of the windows and started trying to prise the shutters open. As she struggled, breaking a fingernail, looking about for some object she could use, running to her handbag and spilling it out for a nail file, a pair of scissors, finding nothing, trying again with her useless fingers, she spoke incessantly, her words coming in little gasps of anger and anxiety.

"Really, one would think that a great man like you could *do* something instead of just standing there. What do you think we shall *do*, just left here in the middle of nowhere after we've come all this way? I can tell you people don't behave like this in England, haven't you got a knife or something? *Un couteau? Un couteau*, for heaven's sake?"

She was almost hysterical. The driver became angry. He picked up her wallet, thrown out of the handbag, and shook it at her. He spoke very quickly. Frightened, she controlled herself. She snatched the wallet from him. She was trembling.

"Very well. Take your money and go." She had not got the exact amount. She gave him two hundred francs. He nodded, looked over the house once more, shrugged his shoulders and moved away.

"The change!" she called. "Change . . ." pronouncing the word, with little hope, in French. *"L' argent . . ."*

"Merci, madame," he said, raising his hand. *"Bonne chance."* He disappeared down the steps. In a moment she saw him walking heavily, not hurrying, across the grass.

"Well," she said, turning to the child. "Well . . ." She paused, listening to the taxi starting up, the sound of its engine revving as it turned in the stony space, departing, diminishing—gone. The child looked at her. Suspicion, for the first time in his life, darkened and swelled his face. It became tumescent, the mouth trembling, the eyes dilated before the moment of tears.

"Let's have some chocolate," she said. The half bar fallen from her handbag had melted completely. "We can't," she said, with a little, brisk laugh. "It's melted."

"Want a drink?"

"A drink." As though in a strange room, she looked around searching for the place where, quite certainly, there must be drink. "Well, I don't know. . ." There was a rusty tap in the wall, presumably used for the hose. She pretended not have seen it. Typhus or worse. She remembered the grapes—they looked far from ripe—that had hung on sagging wires over the steps. "We'll get into the house," she said and added firmly, as though there was no question about it, "We must get in."

"Why can't we go into the house?"

"Because it's locked."

"Where did the people put the key?"

She ran to the door and started searching in the creeper, along the ledge, her fingers recoiling from fear of snakes or lizards. She ran around to the side of the house, the child trotting after her. A makeshift straw roof had been propped up over an old kitchen table. A rusty oil stove stood against the wall of the house. She searched in its greasy oven. She tried the holes in the wall, the dangerous crevices of a giant cactus. The child leaned against the table. He seemed now to be apathetic.

"We'll go around to the back," she said. But at the back of the house there were no windows at all. A narrow gully ran between the house and a steep hill of brown grass. The hill, rising to dense woods, was higher than the roof of the house. She began to climb the hill.

"Don't come," she called. "Stay in the shade."

She climbed backwards, shading her eyes against the unbearable sun. The child sat himself on the wall of the gully, swinging his legs and waiting for her. She looked down on the glistening

113

roof and saw the small mouth of the skylight open. She knew, even while she measured it with her eyes, imagined herself climbing through it, that it was inaccessible. Her mind gabbled unanswerable questions: How far is the nearest house? Telephone? How can we get back to Nice? Where does the road lead to? As she looked down at the house, something swift and black, large as a cat, streaked along the gutter, down the drain-pipe and into the gully.

"Johnny!" she called. "Johnny!" She began to run back down the hill. Her ankle twisted, she fell on the hard grass. She pulled off her sandals and ran barefoot. "Get up from there! Don't sit there!"

"Why?"

"I saw . . ."

"What? What did you see?"

"Oh, nothing. I think we'll have to go back to that house we passed. Perhaps they know . . ."

"What did you see, though?"

"Nothing, nothing. The skylight's open."

"What's a skylight?"

"A sort of window in the roof."

"But what did you *see?*"

"If there was a ladder, perhaps we could . . ." She looked around in a worried way, but without conviction. It was to distract the child from the rat.

"There's a ladder."

It was lying in the gully—a long, strong, new ladder. She looked at it hopelessly, disciplining herself for a blow from fate. "No," she said. "I could never lift it."

The child did not deny this. He asked, "When are the people coming back?"

"I don't know."

"I want some chocolate."

"Oh, Johnny!"

"I want a drink."

"Johnny—*please!*"

"I don't want to be at France. I want to go home now."

"Please, Johnny, you're a big man, you've got to look after Mummy—"

"I don't *want* to—"

"Let's see if we can lift the ladder."

She jumped down into the gully. The ladder was surprisingly light. As she lifted one end, propping the other against the gully wall, juggled it, hand over hand on the rungs, into position, she talked to the child as though he were helping her.

"That's right, it's not a bit heavy, after all, is it, now? Let's just get it straight, that's the way . . ."

Supposing, she thought, the Gachets come back and find me breaking into the house like this? You've paid the rent, she told herself. It's your house. It's scandalous, it's outrageous. One must do *something*.

"Are you going to climb up there?" the child asked, with interest.

She hesitated. "Yes," she said. "Yes, I suppose so."

"Can I go up the ladder too?"

"No, of course not." She grasped the side of the ladder firmly, testing the bottom rung.

"But I *want* to . . ."

"Oh, *Jonathan!* Of course you can't!" she snapped, exasperated. "What d'you think this is—a game? Please, Johnny, *please* don't start. Oh, my God . . ." I *can't* face it, she thought, as she stepped off the ladder, pulled herself up onto the grass, held his loud little body against her sweat-soaked blouse, took off his hat for him and stroked his stubbly hair, rocked him and comforted him, desperately wondered what bribe or reward she might have in her luggage, what prize she could offer. . . . She spoke to him quietly, telling him that if he would let her go up the ladder and get into the house she might find something, she would almost certainly find something, a surprise, a wonderful surprise.

"A toy."

"Well, you never know." She was shameless. "Something really *lovely*."

"A big toy," he stated, knowing his strength.

"A big toy, a lovely bath and a lovely boiled egg—"

"And a biscuit."

"Of course. A chocolate biscuit. And a big glass of milk."

"And two toys. One big and one little."

"Yes, and then we'll go to sleep, and not tomorrow but the next day Daddy will come. . . ." She felt, by the weight against her breast, that she was sending him to sleep. She put him away from her carefully. He lay down, without moving the curled position of his body, on the grass. He sucked his thumb, looking at her out of the corners of his bright eyes. "So I'll climb the ladder. You watch. All right?"

He nodded. She jumped down into the gully again, pulled her tight skirt high above her knees, and started to climb. She kept her eyes away from the gutter. The fear of a rat running close to her made her sick, almost demented with fear. If I see a rat, she thought, I shall jump, I know I shall jump, I can't face it. She saw herself lying dead or unconscious in the gully, the child left completely alone. As she came level with the roof she heard a sound, a quick scuttering; her feet seemed steeped in hot glycerine, her hands weakened. She lay for a moment face downwards on the ladder, certain that when she opened her eyes she would be falling.

When she dared to look again, she was amazed to see how near she was to the skylight—little more than a yard. This distance, certainly, was over burning slate, much of it jagged and broken. But the gutter was firm, and the gradient of the roof very slight. In her relief, now edged with excitement, she did not assess the size of the skylight. The ladder, propped against the gully wall, was steady as a staircase. She mounted two more rungs and cautiously, with one foot, tested the gutter. Now all she had to do was to edge, then fling herself, forward; grasp the sill of the skylight and pull herself up. She did this with a new assurance, almost bravado.

She was already thinking what a story it would be to tell her husband; that her daughters—strong, agile girls—would certainly admire her.

She lay on the roof and looked down through the skylight. It was barely eighteen inches wide—perhaps two feet long. She could no more get through it than a camel through a needle's eye. A child, a thin child, could have managed it. Her youngest daughter could have wormed through somehow. But for her it was impossible.

She looked down at the dusty surface of a chest of drawers. She could almost touch it. Pulling herself forward a little more she could see two doors—attics, no doubt—and a flight of narrow stairs descending into semi-darkness. In her frustration she tried to shake the solid sill of the skylight, as though it might give way. It's not fair, she cried to herself; it's not fair. For a moment she felt like bursting into tears, like sobbing her heart out on the high, hard shoulder of the house. Then, with a kind of delight, she thought—Johnny.

She could lower him through. He would only have to run down the stairs and unbolt one of the downstairs windows. A few weeks ago he had locked himself in the lavatory at home and seemed, for a time, inaccessible. But she had told him what to do, and he had eventually freed himself. Even so, I don't believe you can do this, she told herself. I don't believe you can risk it. At the same time, she knew that she had thought of the obvious—it seemed to her now the only—solution. Her confidence was overwhelming. She was dealing with the situation in a practical, courageous way. She was discovering initiative in herself, and ingenuity.

She came quickly, easily down the ladder. The boy was still curled as she had left him. As she approached, smacking the dust and grime from her skirt, he rolled onto his back, but did not question her. She realized with alarm that he was nearly asleep. A few minutes more and nothing would arouse him. She imagined herself carrying him for miles along the road. Already the heat was thinning. The cicadas, she noticed, were silent.

"Johnny," she said. "Would you like to climb the ladder?"

His eyes focused, but he continued to suck his thumb.

"You can climb the ladder, if you like," she said carelessly.

"Now? Can I climb it now?"

"Yes, if you want to."

"Can I get through the little window?"

She was delighted with him. "Yes. Yes, you can. And, Johnny . . ."

"What?"

"When you've got through the little window, I want you to do something for me. Something very clever. Can you do something clever?"

He nodded, but looked doubtful.

She explained, very carefully, slowly. Then, taking his hand, she led him around to the front of the house. She chose a window so near the ground that he could have climbed through it without effort from the outside. She investigated the shutters, and made certain that they were only held by a hook and eyelet screw on the inside. She told him that he would have to go down two flights of stairs and turn to the right, and he would find the room with the window in it. She tied her handkerchief around his right wrist, so that he would know which way to turn when he got to the bottom of the stairs.

"And if you can't open the window," she said, "you're to come straight back up the stairs. Straight back. And I'll help you through the skylight again. You understand? If you can't open the window, you're to go *straight back* up the stairs. All right?"

"Yes," he said. "Can I climb the ladder now?"

"I'm coming with you. You must go slowly."

But he scaled it like a monkey. She cautioned him, implored him, as she climbed carefully. "Wait, Johnny. Johnny, don't go so fast. Hold on tightly. Johnny, be *careful*. . . ." At the top, she realized that she should have gone first. She had to get around him in order to reach the skylight and pull after her. She was now

118

terribly frightened, and frightened that she would transmit her fear to him. "Isn't it exciting?" she said, her teeth chattering. "Aren't we high up? Now hold on very tightly, because I'm just going to . . ."

She stepped around him. It was necessary this time to put her full weight on the gutter. If I fall, she thought clearly, I must remember to let go of the ladder. The gutter held, and she pulled herself up, sitting quite comfortably on the edge of the skylight. In a moment she had pulled him to her. It was absurdly easy. She put her hands under his arms, feeling the small, separate ribs. He was light and pliable as a terrier.

"Remember what I told you?"

"Yes." He was wriggling, anxious to go.

"What did I tell you?"

"Go downstairs and go that way and open the window."

"And supposing you can't open the window?"

"Come back again."

"And hurry. I'll count. I'll count a hundred. I'll go down and stand by the window. You be there when I've counted a hundred."

"All right," he said.

Holding him tightly in her hands, his legs dangling, his shoulders hunched, she lowered him until he stood safely on the chest of drawers. When she let go, he shook himself and looked up at her.

"Can you get down?" she asked anxiously. "Are you all right?"

He squatted, let his legs down, slid backwards on his stomach and landed with a little thud on the floor.

"It's dirty down here," he said cheerfully.

"Is it all right, though?" She had a new idea, double security. "Run down those stairs and come back, tell me what you see."

Obediently, he turned and ran down the stairs. The moment he had gone, she was panic-stricken. She called, "Johnny! Johnny!" her head through the skylight, her body helpless and unable to

119

follow. "Come back, Johnny! Are you all right?"

He came back almost immediately.

"There's stairs," he said, "going down. Shall I go and open the window now?"

"Yes," she said. "And hurry."

"All right."

"I'm beginning to count now!" And loudly, as she slid back to the ladder, she called, "One . . . two . . . three . . . four . . ." Almost at the bottom, her foot slipped, she tore her skirt. She ran around to the front of the house, and as she came up to the window she began calling again in a bold voice, rough with anxiety. "Forty-nine . . . fifty . . . fifty-one . . ." She hammered with her knuckles on the shutter, shouting. "It's this window, Johnny! Here, Johnny! This one!"

Waiting, she could not keep still. She looked at the split in her skirt, pushed at her straggled hair; she banged again on the shutter; she glanced at her watch; she looked up again and again at the blank face of the house.

"Sixty-eight . . . sixty-nine . . . seventy!"

She sucked the back of her hand, where there was a deep scratch; she folded her impatient arms and unfolded them; she knocked again, calling, "Johnny! Johnny! It's this one!" and then, in a moment, "I've nearly counted a hundred! Are you there, Johnny?"

It's funny, she thought, that the crickets should have stopped. The terrace was now almost entirely in shadow. It gets dark quickly, she remembered. It's not slow. The sun goes, and that's it: It's night-time.

"Ninety . . . ninety-one . . . ninety-two . . . Johnny? Come on. Hurry up!"

Give him time, she told herself. He's only five. He never can hurry. She went and sat on the low wall at the edge of the terrace. She watched the minute-hand of her watch creeping across the seconds. Five minutes. It must be five minutes. She stood up, cupping her hands around her mouth.

"A hundred!" she shouted. "I've counted a hundred!"

An aeroplane flew high, high overhead, where the sky was the most delicate blue. It made no sound. There was no sound. As though she were suddenly deaf she reached, stretched her body, made herself entirely a receptacle for sound—a snapping twig, a bird hopping; even a fall of dust. The house stood in the front of her like a locked box. The sunlight at the end of the terrace went out.

"Johhhn-ny! I'm here! I'm down here!"

She managed to get two fingers in the chink between the shutters. She could see the rusty arm of the hook. But she could not reach it. The shutters had warped, and the aperture at the top was too small for anything but a knife, a nail file, a piece of tin.

"I'm going back up the ladder!" she shouted. "Come back to the skylight! Do you hear me?"

One cicada began its noise again, only one. She ran around to the back of the house and for the third time climbed the ladder, throwing herself without caution onto the roof, dragging herself to the open skylight. There was a wide track in the dust, where he had slid off the chest of drawers.

"Johnny! Johnny! Where are you!"

Her voice was deadened by the small, enclosed landing. It was like shouting into the earth. There was no volume to it, and no echo. Without realizing it, she had begun to cry. Her head lowered into the almost total darkness, she sobbed, "Johnny! Come up here! I'm here by the skylight, by the little window!"

In the silence she heard, quite distinctly, a tap dripping. A regular, metallic drip, like torture. She shouted directions to him, waiting between each one, straining to hear the slightest sound, the faintest answer. The tap dripped. The house seemed to be holding its breath.

"I'm going down again! I'm going back to the window!"

She wrestled once more with the shutters. She found a small stick, which broke. She poked with her latch-key, with a comb. She dragged the table across the terrace and tried, standing on it, to reach the first-floor windows. She climbed the ladder twice more, each time expecting to find him under the skylight, waiting for her.

It was now dark. Her strength had gone and her calls became feeble, delivered brokenly, like prayers. She ran around the house, uselessly searching and shouting his name. She threw a few stones at the upper windows. She fell on the front door, kicking it with her bare feet. She climbed the ladder again and this time lost her grip on the gutter and only just saved herself from falling. As she lay on the roof, she became dizzy and frightened, in some part of her, that she was going to faint. The other part of her didn't care. She lay for a long time with her head through the skylight, weeping and calling, sometimes weakly, sometimes with an attempt at command; sometimes, with a desperate return of will, trying to force herself through the impossible opening.

For the last time, she beat on the shutters, her blows as puny as his would have been. It was three hours since she had lowered him through the skylight. What more could she do? There was nothing more she could do. At last she said to herself, something has happened to him, I must go for help.

It was terrible to leave the house. As she stumbled down the steps and across the grass, which cut into her feet like stubble, she kept looking back, listening. Once she imagined she heard a cry, and ran back a few yards. But it was only the cicada.

It took her a long time to reach the road. The moon had risen. She walked in little spurts, running a few steps, then faltering, almost loitering until she began to run again. She remembered the pink house in the vineyard. She did not know how far it was; only that it was before the woods. She was crying all the time now, but did not notice it, any more than she was aware of her curious, in fact alarming, appearance. "Johnny!" she kept sobbing. "Oh, Johnny." She began to trot, keeping up an even pace. The road rose and fell; over each slope she expected to see the lights of the pink house. When she saw the headlamps of a car bearing down on her, she stepped into the middle of the road and beat her arms up and down, calling, "Stop! Stop!"

The car swerved to avoid her, skidded, drew up with a scream across the road. She ran towards it.

"Please! . . . Please!"

The faces of the three men were shocked and hostile. They began to shout at her in French. Their arms whirled like propellers. One shook his fist.

"Please . . ." she gasped, clinging to window. "Do you speak English? Please do you speak English?"

One of the men said. "A little." The other two turned on him. There was uproar.

"Please. I beg of you. It's my little boy." Saying the words, she began to weep uncontrollably.

"An accident?"

"Yes, yes. In the house, up there. I can't get into the house—"

It was a long, difficult time before they understood; each amazing fact had to be interpreted. If it had been their home, they might have asked her in; at least opened the door. She had to implore and harangue them through a half-open window. At last the men consulted together.

"My friends say we cannot . . . enter this house. They do not wish to go to prison."

"But it's *my* house—I've paid for it!"

"That may be. We do not know."

"Then take me to the police—take me to the British Consul—"

The discussion became more deliberate. It seemed that they were going to believe her.

"But how can we get in? You say the house is locked up. We have no tools. We are not—"

"A hammer would do—if you had a hammer and chisel—"

They shook their heads. One of them even laughed. They were now perfectly relaxed, sitting comfortably in their seats. The interpreter lit a cigarette.

"There's a farm back there," she entreated. "It's only a little way. Will you take me? Please, please, will you take me?"

The interpreter considered this, slowly breathing smoke, before even putting it to his friends. He looked at his flat, black-faced, illuminated watch. Then he threw the question to them out of the corner of his mouth. They made sounds of doubt, weighing the possibility, the inconvenience.

"Johnny may be dying," she said. "He must have fallen. He must be hurt badly. He may"—her voice rose, she shook the window—"he may be dead. . . ."

They opened the back door and let her into the car.

"Turn around," she said. "It's back there on the left. But it's away from the road, so you must look out."

In the car, since there was nothing she could do, she began to shiver. She realized for the first time her responsibility. I may have murdered him. The feeling of the child as she lifted him through the skylight came back to her hands: his warmth. The men, embarrassed, did not speak.

"There it is! There!"

They turned off the road. She struggled from the car before it had stopped, and ran to the front door. The men in the car waited, not wishing to compromise themselves, but curious to see what was going to happen.

The door was opened by a small woman in trousers. She was struck by the barrage of words, stepped back from it. Then, with her myopic eyes, she saw the whole shape of distress—a person in pieces. "My dear," she said. "My dear . . . what's happened? What's the matter?"

"You're English? Oh—you're English?"

"My name's Pat Jardine. Please come in, please let me do something for you—" Miss Jardine's handsome little face was overcast with pain. She could not bear suffering. Her house was full of cats; she made splints for sparrows out of matchsticks. If her friend Yvonne killed a wasp, Miss Jardine turned away, shutting her eyes tight and whispering, "Oh, the poor darling." As she listened to the story her eyes filled with tears, but her mind with purposes.

124

"We have a hammer, chisel, even a crowbar," she said. "But the awful thing is, we haven't a man. I mean, of course we can try—we *must* try—but it would be useful to have a man. Now who can I—?"

"There are three men in the car, but they don't speak English and they don't—"

Miss Jardine hurried to the car. She spoke quietly but passionately, allowing no interruption. Another woman appeared, older, at first suspicious.

"Yvonne," Miss Jardine said, breathlessly introducing her. "Get the crowbar, dear, and the hammer—and perhaps the axe, yes, get the axe—" At the same time she poured and offered a glass of brandy. "Drink this. What else do we need? Blankets. First-aid box. You never know."

"Thank you. Thank you."

"Nonsense, I'm only glad you came to us. Now we must go. Yvonne? Have you got the axe, dear?"

The three men had got out of the car and were standing about. They looked, in their brilliant shirts and pointed shoes, their slight glints of gold and chromium, like women on a battlefield— at a loss. Yvonne and Miss Jardine clattered the great tools into the boot of the car. Miss Jardine hurried away for a rope. The men murmured together, and laughed quietly and self-consciously. When everything was ready they got into the car. The three women squeezed into the back.

On the way, driving fast, eating up the darkness, Miss Jardine said, "But I simply don't understand the Gachets. If they knew you were coming today. I mean, it's simply scandalous."

"They are decadent people," Yvonne said slowly. "They have been spoiled, pigging it in that house all winter. The owners take no interest, now their children are grown up. The Gachets did not wish to work for you, obviously."

"But at least they could have *said*—"

"They are decadent people," Yvonne repeated. After a half a mile, she added, "Gachet drinks two litres of wine a day. His wife is Italian."

Now there were so many people. The hours of being alone were over. But she could not speak. She sat forward on the seat, her hands tightly clasped, her face shrivelled. When they came to the turning, she opened her lips and took a breath, but Miss Jardine had already directed them. They lurched and bumped up the lane, screamed to a stop in front of the black barn doors.

"Is that locked too?" Yvonne asked.

There was no answer. They clambered out. Yvonne gave the tools and the rope to the men. Yvonne and Miss Jardine carried the blankets and the first-aid box.

"A torch," Miss Jardine said. "Blast!"

"We have a light," the interpreter said. "Although it does not seem necessary."

"Good. Then let's go."

She ran in front of them, although there was no purpose in reaching the house first. It was so clear in the moonlight she could see the things spilled out of her handbag, the mirror of her powder compact, the brass catch of her purse. Before she was up the steps, she began to call again, "Johnny? Johnny?" The others, coming more slowly behind her with their burdens, felt pity, reluctance and dread.

"What shall we try first? The door?"

"No, we'll have to break a window. The door's too solid."

"Which of you can use an axe?"

The men glanced at each other. Finally the interpreter shrugged his shoulders and took the axe, weighing it. Yvonne spoke contemptuously to him, making as though to take the axe herself. He went up to the window, raised the axe and smashed it into the shutters. Glass and wood splintered. It had only needed one blow.

She was at the window, tugging at the jagged edges of the glass. The interpreter pushed her out of the way. He undid the latch of the window and stood back, examining a small scratch on his wrist and shaking his hand in the air as though to relieve some intolerable hurt. She was through the window, blundering across a room, while she heard Miss Jardine calling, "Open the front door if you can! We're coming!"

They did not exist for her any longer. She did not look for light switches. The stairs were brilliant.

"Johnny?" she called. "Johnny? Where are you?"

A door on the first-floor landing was wide open. She ran to the doorway and her hands, without any thought from herself, flew out and caught the lintel on either side, preventing her entrance.

He was lying on the floor. He was lying in exactly the same position in which he had curled on the grass outside, except that his thumb had fallen from his mouth; but it was still upright, still wet. His small snores came rhythmically, with a slight click at the end of each snore. Surrounding him was a confusion, a Christmas of toys. In his free hand he had been holding a wooden soldier; it was still propped inside the lax, curling fingers. She was aware, in a moment of absolute detachment, that the toys were very old; older possibly, than herself. Then she stopped thinking. She walked forward.

Kneeling, she touched him. He mumbled, but did not wake up. She shook him, quite gently. He opened his eyes directly on to her awful, hardly recognizable face.

"I like the toys," he said. His thumb went back into his mouth. His eyelids sank. His free hand gripped the soldier, then loosened.

"*Jonathan!*"

With one hand she pushed him upright. With the other, she hit him. She struck him so hard that her palm stung.

One of the women started screaming. "Oh, no! . . . No!"

She struggled to her feet and pushed past the blurred, obstructing figure in the doorway. She stumbled down the stairs. The child was crying. The dead house was full of sound. She flung herself into a room. "Oh, thank God," she whispered. "Oh, thank God. . . ." She crouched with her head on her knees, her arms wrapped around her own body, her body rocking with the pain of gratitude.

D.C. PUBLIC LIBRARY

3 1172 01471 0107

POP.

The Public Library
of the
District of Columbia
Washington, D.C.

P.L. 117 revised

MARTIN LUTHER KING LIBRARY

Theft or mutilation
is punishable by law